WEST OF SPENCER

R A BARD

TO SENANG HATI
AND HER EXCEPTIONALLY SYMPATHETIC
OWNERS MIKE & CARROL

IN FRIENDSHIP,

RICHARD

 ISBN 978-0615748450
Published Jan. 2013 by Smooth Passage Books

Cover: detail of "Trolling for Kings" by Tom Teitge

It was not supposed to end like this. Not mired in pain, fully aware as life slips away, slowly and inexorably as the stars creeping across the sky.

Yeah, we always said we wanted to die in the trolling hatch, with our boots on, we loved our work that much. But the image remained undeveloped. If we ever thought more deeply about it, the end we imagined would have been sudden: a quickly obliterating heart attack, or a fatal slip overboard into icy water. And certainly only at the end of a long, satisfying life. Not with a heart still full of hunger, still able to see the future filled with love and lust and friendship, struggle and reward and hope...hope that with the passing hours becomes less and less justified.

The stars, and then the sun, and the stars again, above the vast ocean. Ample time to ponder what lies beyond the horizon. But nowhere near enough information. All is theory, all is unknowable, all is despair and perhaps the end will be a merciful release from ignorance, from regret over missed opportunity and errors of judgment....

The sun once again, now obscured. Wind beginning to rise. Murmur of the first small waves at the waterline.

PART ONE

Sitka

CHAPTER 1

A stray sunray burns through the Baranof Island cloud cover and rakes the vacant lot across from the gear store, quick slash of green brilliance in the roadside thicket of salmonberry. Glints off the door mirror of a rusting 1985 Oldsmobile jacked up on blocks and across the face of a form laid out in the back seat. Modulation of loud snoring.

Bo waking to the mixed aroma of aged vinyl and chicken droppings, the vehicle a favored roost by neighbors' flock. If not in use by Bo when experience tells him he would not be lovingly welcomed at home of landlady.

As for example after last night. Polynesian Friday at the Quixote Club, Bo arriving early to find a seat beneath a plastic palm tree and take advantage of a special on Longboard lager and well tequila. Quest for oblivion soon accomplished, the evening slipping into a comfortable alcoholic funk as the crowd swells and ebbs, couples lurching across a tiny open space to sound of an ad hoc trio loosely interpreting Jimmy Buffett —my God, that is Rick off the Gertie, large bare belly bulging above grass skirt, thumping a ukulele.

—Is this seat open?

Tall sleek female of impressive decolletage pulling an empty chair close, giving a name Myra before launching into a stupefyingly encyclopedic history of clerical employment in Great Falls preceding this new job as business and canine interest reporter for the Watchdog. Bo soon passing coherence, able only to adopt an attentive pose and nod, possibly at appropriate times, at this vision of long dark brown tressed beauty.

—Oh it's late I promised a friend we'd have a nightcap at the Shee Attika.

Bo left to muse on the squeezing together and positioning of breasts behind plunging necklines…it could be seen as friendly invitation…rude, perhaps, to resist the impulse to reach right in and get acquainted?

— Actually, it's pronounced pango pango

Festering disagreement between gillnetter and seine crewman at the bar intruding on Bo's reverie.

—What? Like I said, if you go down there in the winter after albacore, you can deliver into Pago Pago—

—Pango pango.

—And if your load is big enough they give you—

—Pango pango

—two nights at the Sadie Thompson—

—Pango pango.

—Hey! Shut the fuck up! Nobody asked you into this conversation. It's pay-go pay-go. Dickhead.

—The hell do you know about it you've probably never been south of Cape Addington.

—You're the geography expert? Seattle jerks, coming up to hoover our salmon after you smother all yours on the lower coast in PCBs and cowshit.

—Smother this, asshole.

The principals' friends joining in, jostling, spilling out to the parking lot where a few perfunctory punches are thrown as Herman the bartender guides Bo too out the door.

—Closing time man we'll see you next time.

Bo setting off on the three mile bicycle ride back to town, a venture clearly destined to fail. Standing perplexed in the ditch after a second tumble. The benevolent seine crew giving him a ride in back of pickup, happily bouncing over potholes in the light rain to lean bike on bashed fender and nod off on the pliant Cutlass upholstery.

Now, loud screech of rusting hinges as he pushes a back door open, stretches throbbing head out, a wave of nausea about to erupt when he notices inches from his nose a home-inked "Jesus" tattooed on a sturdy ankle. Recognizable even in his stuporous state as belonging to Effie Hudson, a no nonsense woman whose right-of-way is respected by all including her husband Albert, affable vice president of the local Alaska Native Brotherhood chapter. A voice tromboning from above.

—Not on my turnips, Bo. You go barf out the other side of your car.

Bo invoking the name of the Tatooed under his breath. Though this is not an unreasonable request. Considering the Olds is placed perilously close to the lot line, and thus encroaches on the rows of vegetables Effie intimidates into rising from the ground in great healthy profusion.

And so Bo, though no lover of turnips, pulls shut the door and struggles to reverse his position. Which effort eases the unhappiness in his gut and allows him to sit more or less upright. And entertain a restorative vision of eggs. Hashbrowns. Coffee. Emerging creakily from the car's south side, tentatively stretching, blessed by another wash of sunlight. The day's promise coming to focus. I bet I could get to the Lincoln without falling off my bike.

Prudently walking the Bobcat down the steep rocky cut to the sidewalk to mount and pedal along Katlian Street through soft damp Sitka air past piles of stowed crab pots and longline drums, through the roar of fans and clatter of forklifts from the Southeast Seafoods plant, scraps of Spanish as the head-and-gut crew hangs with cell phones deployed, smoking and jiving on the 10 a.m. break in slimestreaked Hellies.

Propping bike against café front window to pull door open on this warm…

Picking bike up and repropping it.

…this warm dark welcoming haven for drunks

and fishermen. Strangely unpopulated for a Saturday morning. Bo sliding into a vinyl seat adjacent to the only other occupied booth after glancing approvingly at the gently snoring supine figure of Bill Sheridan, publisher of the Watchdog and police radio junkie. Whose addiction is known to peak late Friday nights when the law is most likely to be disrespected by inebriates, bangers, and excitable dogs, providing a rich vein of material for the Monday edition.

—How's it going Bo?

Familiar friendly voice of Trish the waitress who takes Bo's order and brings back eggs and potatoes to be smothered with catsup and devoured with gusto, on the second coffee refill asking offhand,

—How come you're not fishing, made enough money already this year?

—What do you mean fishing?

—You didn't know, Fish and Game made a last minute announcement yesterday, says there's a lot of hatchery fish around. They're opening the inside up for two days. It started at 12:01 this morning, Bo, that's why there's nobody in here.

—Holy shit! How come I'm still here, then?

—Well...

A fond tolerant smile

—I thought you weren't one of those strivers.

—Yeah well...that was before the dock price went through the roof.

The leftover alcoholic fog dissipates as urgent pre-departure thoughts jostle in Bo's mind. Hold, still two thirds full of ice, should be workable but may need some chopping. Fuel topped off after last trip, food, I can live off the backup canned stuff for a few days, gear still all tied up and ready to go in the trolling hatch. Deckhand—Reilly's still in Flagstaff till next week...but company would be nice...this last engendered by sight of Trish reaching for roll of paper towels on high shelf exposing slice of midriff and eliciting a pleasant memory of several autumns ago when the slow fishing allowed an occasional lazy morning at anchor off the hot spring out past Peisar Island. But better now to make this short trip without distractions.

Bill paid, Bo pushing out the Lincoln's door to find the street transformed by a whorling mass of tourists lightered in from the cruise ship anchored out in the bay, flooding in blinking oddly dressed profusion down Lincoln St. around both sides of the old Orthodox church that splits the avenue just like, Bo now thinks, the way the traffic flowed around the high walled cemetery in the Piazale Donatello where it splits the Viale Matteotti...not far from where Mariella's dark hair coursed over her shoulder, lovely breasts in profile as she stood at the window in soft afternoon light looking past the courtyard treetops toward the Arno after lovemaking made reckless by the as yet unvoiced imminent end of their life together—familiar deep seated pain rising and eyes starting to sting—my God! to still be wracked like this after seven months what misanthrope designed us to be so vulnerable, that One in the Judgment Day fresco in the cathedral dome surrounded by his pious flock complacently overseeing the diabolical action below, that sounds about right…

The door still ajar, Bo wavering, then turning to retrace steps past counter. Ignoring significant look from Trish and entering a small dark space opening from the back of the café. Eight stools, cracked mirror behind a worn wood bar, gloomy Red looking up from whatever he's reading beneath a dim lamp.

—By God it's a customer. Rocks this morning, Bo?

—No, straight's fine thanks.

The whisky coursing from the bottle mouth out the silver tube, glass placed before Bo who eyes it a moment before taking a long swallow. Heat descending below and above, promise of relief. But a dissenting thought. What the fuck am I doing. The opener. Late but plenty of time to perhaps find some fish. Leave this self pity. I'm capable?

Another long stare at the amber liquid, then standing, laying bill on the bar. And again out the door. Okay. Get on bike and get your ass going. Yes this is better. A narrow escape but I made it. Pump up the hill, quick detour to Karen's before heading for the harbor.

No response to shouted hello, finding an envelope in the trash to scribble

K—fishing opened up see you in a couple days?

Attacking the unpaved track above the Pioneer Bar now hangover-free and fearless, round stones popping out from under the tires, turning to pass my good old Cutlass and on to the sidewalk, through the parking lot and the ramp down to the floats giving a congenial fuck you as always to the 'no bicycles' sign.

Six fingers down F float to the Walter K snugged starboard side to, Bo stepping over the gunwale and aft to slide open the door and step into the wheelhouse. Light scent of diesel layering over an evocation of fish coming from the hanging locker and its drying oilskins. And the less perceptible sweet tone of bilge rising from the engine room. Down into which Bo now climbs to check dipstick, expansion tank, and bilge level, finding all satisfactory and reascending to push the starter and listen to the Cummins clear its throat and idle to smoothness.

The wind light and conducive to an easy exit, Bo pulls the mooring lines onto the boat and reverses into the fairway, coasting back toward the Heritage, Al Hudson's seiner. Residual twinge of nausea as the image of Effie's ankle briefly reappears. Cranking the wheel hard right and goosing the engine to bring the bow around to the basin entrance. Noting, most slips occupied by trollers now empty. Out the channel, curving around Battery Island and past the green can and the last rock barely showing awash now and then in an easy swell.

A couple of trollers hull down to the west, the Vs of their tall poles angled out in fishing position. Momentarily clear of hazards, Bo engages the autopilot and steps out to loosen the port haulup line, braces against the cabin and uses his butt to start the tall fir pole swinging out of the crosstree. Letting the lines slip through toughened hands till the pole reaches a 45-degree angle and he can jam the rollback preventer down.

Repeating on the starboard side. Now we look like business.

Back in the wheelhouse, VHF on the weather channel, Bo's heart sinking. No wind over 10 knots for the next three days…seas less than five feet…my God we're cursed with clemency, now everyone and his nephew will be out there along the line between St. Lazaria and Biorka. Fifty boats scuffling to get as near as possible to the off-limits outside zone where most of the fish will be. A zoo. Yucking at the image, Bo grabs the tide table. Hmm. Ebb's four days after its peak. Salisbury Sound could be fat…it's a gamble…but what's the risk anyway with this late start. The hot fishing at the Cape's probably over already with all that effort, now they'll just be fighting over the crumbs. Yep this is the best way to go.

Cutting the pilot to turn north, familiar mix of hope and dread whenever Bo breaks away from the presumed wisdom of the fleet. Back outside to coil and lash the mooring lines to cleats on the hatch cover, taking a moment to turn pale face to sun as it enters a big cloud window, eyes closed to soak in the bright red eyelid warmth before it fades to orange and then brown.

Following the familiar course through Olga and Neva Straits, Bach and the Brandenbergs dialed into the headphones in hopes of transport during the three hour run. When not avoiding oncoming tugs in the narrow cuts. Or watching the high speed tourist boats rush past like a modern troop carrier fleet, their target the sea otter population of Salisbury Sound, numbers thinning before the onslaught of rumbling diesels—

Enough grumbling. Better to concentrate on these swelling chords from the string section…

Past St. John the Baptist Bay and out along the first likely stretch of shore, eyes intent on the sounder looking for bait sign. The screen blank blue above a scrolling black bottom line…fighting off panicky thoughts. If this place proves dead? Slink back to the Cape? Preserve me from that…no. It won't be. All blue past two more rocky points and then here's a good size ball of bait showing, one or two more and the screen fills solid red and black from fifteen fathoms down to forty. Urgency rising, get the gear into the water! No be patient let's plot the extent of this school…two minutes more at running speed before it ends, Jesus this thing is big, I'll just u-turn down here and the gear should be mostly in by the time I cross into it again.

Wheeling and throttling down to two knots. Switching on the hydraulics, stowing the cockpit covers and climbing down into the hatch—here we go then. Stack the flashers, ready to toss out as the stainless wire spools down. Snapping the bottom spoon on just above a heavy lead cannonball, Bo turns the hydraulic lever and lifts the 45-pound lead weight out of its holder, pushes it out past the rail and starts it down at medium speed, snapping a flasher or spoon leader onto the wire every three fathoms.

Five spreads down and the line jerks back. Bo's hand on the wire, the familiar glorious sensation—it is by God a fish this soon, a big king by the feel of it. Oh Lady of unexpected fortune would you be sailing with me today.

Temptation to pull the salmon filling Bo's veins like a drug—but I scorn the lure of short term profit, I will finish lowering this line to forty fathoms, and I will attach its float and let it drift back while I set the other float line, and then I will do the same with the two deep lines and then I will prove the depth of my will power by drinking a Pepsi before I start hauling.

This resolve lasting through exactly one swig. Bells on the ends of the trolling poles ringing a symphony of struggle as hooked fish jerk hard against the 100-pound-test leaders. Bo begins spooling in the insistently twitching deep line. Fish number one on the top spread. Bo takes the snap off the wire and fixes it to a line on the hatch combing before hand over handing the three-fathom leader in, gaff ready in right hand, pulling when the fish rests and stopping or slipping it out when it fights, finally when it's just below him swings the gaff down hard on the top of its head. The stunned salmon rolls on its side, gill cover gasping open, Bo working the gaff's stainless hook in past the gills lifts the deep purple-backed silvery creature up over the rail and onto the deck, one more blow with the gaff before slipping a blade in just below the gill to let the dark red blood pool out across the light gray deck.

Holding the leader taut, Bo works the gaff into the curve of the hook and pulls it out of the fish's mouth with a quick jerk, then sets the flasher aside and resumes spooling in the wire. On the next hook another salmon. This one is tired and comes along easily, but Bo thunks it to prevent any sudden explosive revival before landing it next to what looks like its twin brother.

On the next hook another fish and on the next another and on until as the line is back down and swinging out to trail behind the pole tip seven fat twenty-pound kings fill the port checker.

The float line yields a similar abundance as does the starboard deep, and Bo begins running on adrenaline and endorphins and the afternoon turns dreamlike. A waking dream, attention needed to stay on the depth contour and in the feed, but a dream nonetheless because this is the ideal every fisherman hopes will come his way to make up for the desolate fishless days...the breakdowns...the enervating rough weather...all distant negligible worries now.

Cloud cover obscuring the sun and now a southerly breeze comes up accompanied by light rain. Eliciting thanks from Bo, since now he can stop hosing the fish which have spilled over the checker boards and are piling up alongside the cabin. And maybe hold off cleaning them for another hour. Since this kind of fishing can't go on forever, the pace just as likely to drop to nothing at any time. So I will just go through the gear one more time and then I will dress the first ones that came aboard and get them down onto the ice. Out of how may already landed. My God there must be fifty fish here. Oh now you have gone and done it. Got yourself into the sweetest spot and not another boat in sight.

These thoughts vague riders on the surface of Bo's immersion in hunter instinct, along with awareness of an arm beginning to ache and the far off memory that was breakfast but content to be so occupied as to deny their relevance.

Four more lines up and down, twenty more fish, and then the shoal of feed fish disappears from the sounder's screen as abruptly and completely as if a vacuum had sucked it into another dimension. Bo runs two lines for three weary salmon and puts the boat on a long westward tack. Maybe they all just slid this way. Although more likely the herring school went deep or finally realized what was happening and spread out to avoid total decimation.

But whatever. I'll just set up the cleaning trough and get to work on this first fish. A curving slice frees the gills to be tossed overboard, then the smooth slit from vent to collar, a cut around the gut's attachment and the whole set of entrails lifts out—slice down the blood cavity and scoop out that congealed kidney skein, squeeze the blood in the belly veins toward the spine and free, a rinse with the deck hose and set the fish aside for a final rinse later before scooting it up the deck toward the fish hold.

Into a rhythm. Gills and guts flying overboard. The deck filling with blood and gurry, hose running to keep it all moving toward the scuppers. Stopping now and then to hopefully run a line. Mid evening hitting a solitary feed ball that produces a dozen fish. But nothing on the back tack. And then more nothing until the last pull at dark, when three sundowners climb on.

Bo making a long run back into St. John the Baptist for its good holding bottom. And superior protection. Not that there's any weather expected. But still. The anchor set in sticky sand in eight fathoms, Bo empties two big cans of Dinty Moore beef stew into a pot to simmer while he cleans the last fish and lowers them into the hold to join a huge stack of their fellows. Gratefully sitting down to a steaming bowl, trying not to get too comfortable on the settee cushion. So as not to fall asleep exhausted and miss the chance to spend two hours layering fish and ice into the bins below. I will be working until one a.m. but so what. I can do that and I will get up at three to see if that feed has risen. Jesus I caught more than ninety fish today. I am a fishing machine. And one lucky son of a bitch. Thank you Dinty Moore. Dump this bowl and pot in the sink and move on to my pressing appointment with some dead salmon.

Two hours later Bo climbs out of the hold, hangs his oilskins, leaves his rank clothes in a pile, sets two alarm clocks for 2:45 crawls gratefully into his bunk and falls instantly asleep.

CHAPTER 2

The first alarm is a rather harmonious bell and it is the second's irritating buzz that works. What is that Jesus it's still dark I could lie here a little longer but no it's an hour before I can get out to the drag and put the gear in and any bite will be starting soon. I can do this one more day it's only nineteen hours until it's dark again and then I can rest unless I catch another mass of fish like I did yesterday and that would be all right too.

Fighting an urge to fire up immediately Bo drops into the engine room to check oil and water. Then with the Cummins at fast idle steps blearily onto the foredeck to watch in the dim light the anchor chain spooling onto the winch's drum. Clanking of links coming over the roller waking him up a bit. Occasionally stomping on the chain between roller and winch to shake the muddy sand off. Stopping the winch after the last ten feet of extra heavy chain has rattled up and the anchor is snugged tight against the roller and the dog set.

Roaring out of the Bay at 1900 revs and 8 knots,

not fuel efficient but there are fish out there waiting for my lurid display of chrome shiny bronze and bright plastic.

One hopes.

Heading out along the Sound's rocky south shore. We'll go to the closure line and troll back from there. In case the prey/predator community has strayed that way.

Slowing and throwing out lures half a mile from the spot so as to start the drag fully armed. Just at the line Bo wheels in a wide semicircle and trolls back east. With no lines having jerked during deployment. And no bells now ringing. Well. I guess I can make some coffee.

Legs dangling in the trolling hatch with the first best mug of the day. Still twenty minutes till sunup, but the trees on shore and the small rocky islets out by the mouth of the Sound now well defined. Clouded over but calm and no rain. Yet. And in the air that mix of spruce forest and living ocean. That if you could figure out how to package it—

—Yow what the fuck

The starboard pole rattling and shaking all the way down to its pivot on the rail, holy shit did I snag bottom what's the depth Jesus, no it's still deep but look at that float, bouncing up and down like a rodeo bull. Still no sign of feed on the meter. But it may be close by. I'll just step in here and put a mark on the plotter and pull on these—whewf—rain pants and then I believe I will get to work. After I put an edge on this knife. To let Mr. Monster mellow out a bit.

Finally engaging the gurdy and starting the line in. Nothing on the top leader. Nor on the second. But here he comes. One surmises from the sudden upwelling in the calm water twenty feet back. Bo pulls out the ring end of a long stretchy rubber snubber fixed to the inside of the hatch and carefully resnaps the leader onto it. Okay now. Jesus it's like a log. Two hands then. Haul with full strength and get a new purchase. One foot at a time. Divided into eighteen feet is. Oof that's not even six inches. But here he comes again. Slow steady progress. My God I've never seen a salmon that big. He must be seventy pounds. And still no struggle Keep that thought. Almost here. Where's my gaff. Now stop showing your chin. It's the top of your head I need. Maybe a tug in closer to the boat—

—Oh no no noooo

Suddenly freaking, the giant king turns yanks the leader out of Bo's hand and streaks wide with a force that would have snapped the monofilament but the snubber stretches twice its length and holds. Okay come back in here you're tired let's get this over with. Hand over hand again, trying to keep the gathered leader from snarling, slowly gaining until here he is again, right side up this time. Bo swings savagely and the king's mouth sags open showing a big black tongue and an alligator's worth of teeth. Two more cracks on top of head to make sure. Turning the gaff and sinking the sharp curved hook deep into the tougher flesh just above the eye. Hauling with the added strength of pure desire, yarding the fish up and sliding it over the rail and onto the deck my God that is a big fish.

Bo cuts the artery starting a gush of blood and sits back on the hatch cover only now aware of the race of his heartbeat. Irridescent shine slowly fading from the scaly surface as the life leaves—this makes me happy and sorrowful at the same time how can that be. No answer to this question but there are more fish on the lines. Excuse me your excellency while I retrieve this hook from your mouth. And start the wire in again. Look at that there's another fish. Maybe fifteen pounds, a sardine in comparison. But who's complaining.

Bo finishes the deep and runs through the other three lines for twelve fish. After that the pace settles to a slower but steady rate of two or three per wire. Although no feed shows on the sounder. But the herring must still be somewhere around here to hold these salmon. Or maybe it's my gear they're following. Dozens of shiny lures wiggling along giving every indication of a school of baitfish, perhaps. Or perhaps not. I am not a trained fish psychologist. But I am happy with this fishing. It could be faster but on the other hand I can keep up with the cleaning. Which will make Art at the plant happy. As he goes sticking his temperature probe into the bellies of my iced fish to ensure they're worthy of the snootiest New York restaurant.

At just before noon the bite abruptly stops as if a valve has turned off. It's over. Might as well pull the gear aboard and head for Sitka. Not that midday isn't always the slow time, when everything in the natural world too seems to favor a siesta. After the fish take their post-lunch nap the tide could shift, the herring could surface, it could be just as hot as it was yesterday, remember I didn't even start till two. This is the last day, I can't give up early.

Perking up around four the fish stage a three hour slow-paced revival before shutting down again. With no late evening clatter. This bite's on the downturn, I can declare with assurance. Since no one will be here tomorrow to prove me wrong.

With the gear stowed on board and the Walter apparently the only boat in the universe, Bo angles away from the beach on autopilot and jumps down into the hold to ice the last few fish of the afternoon. Hacking at a remnant block to free enough flakes to pack their bellies and cover them once they're layered atop their fellows in the aft bin. Then back up into the falling dark to run with radar and plotter through narrowing channel toward John the Baptist. Which I could pass by and in another four hours be tied up in Thompson Harbor. The point of which would be what exactly. Better to go in here and bed down with these clams than to run exhausted through the night.

CHAPTER 3

Waking late morning, Bo motors to Sitka to radio the fish plant and get a place at the end of a long list of other trollers waiting to offload. Just outside the Thompson breakwater, a fit of dithering setting in. All these kings on board…this is a rare feeling of accomplishment…if I go in and tie up it will surely be diluted by the usual blather and everyone will want to tell me how many more kings they caught on *their* biggest day ever. Maybe better to toss the anchor out here and savor the high, settle in with a pot of spiced tea and afternoon jazz on WKAT and allow myself some pride in what I have encased in ice under the hatch cover. Jesus, this is almost more than I've ever made for a full trip. Thank you, herring, for attracting those kings to my little spot…dozing off to be waked in darkness by the dock foreman's voice on the radio.

—*Walter K-- Southeast Seafoods.*

—Walter K back.

—*You're up, hoist # 3*

—Roger, I'm on my way.

Bo gets a midships line around a piling, squints up against the big floods that form a bright envelope of light around the Walter in the otherwise dark channel. The normally impassive hoist operator staring down, double-taking.

—How many you say again?

—190, about.

Cleating the line, Bo shifts aft to lead a stern line forward around another pile to snug the boat so the hoist arm will clear the mast.

—Okay Dave we're good.

The arm swings out and, winch motor whining, lowers the two by four foot aluminum bucket to where Bo can guide it through the open hatch to land with a heavy clank. Dropping down after it to kick loose the ice-encased fish in the port bin and count them into the bucket. One, two, three... ...seventeen...twenty-nine

—Okay Dave let's go up.

Muscling the rising bucket until it clears the coaming, Bo grabs the snow shovel and pitches ice up and out until the center's cleared for the bucket's return. Who's next then. How about you in the back with just your tail sticking out. A bit recalcitrant are we. A boot heel to loosen the ice cube around your head and here we come. Thirty-two in this bucket...twenty-six in the next...and here now taking up almost half of the front crossing is Ms. Monster, nestled among a bunch of smaller fish like a sow and piglets. What a beast. Bo remembering the heavy egg skeins, not yet ripe despite her massive size. How big would she have been at maturity. Enough to feed the most generous wedding party with all the grand uncles and third cousins twice removed.

Two more hoists and the last of the salmon climb heavenward. Bo takes the shovel and goes aerobic with the remaining half ton of blood-infused ice, pitching it up onto the deck to hose off later. Interrupted by Dave's call.

—Ready for weigh-up Bo if you want to climb out.

Bo standing next to the scale trying to stay attentive to the numbers as a forklift driver in fluorescent green oilskins deposits and withdraws blue totes filled with the various grades of his salmon. The young checker's Slavic accent providing some interest but Bo finding even more distracting the blood smear on his neck. That there is the exact shape of Kentucky. I wonder if Lexington has a big Ukrainian population. I wonder how many continents worth of blood smears I'm displaying. Boy a shower's going to feel good.

—You have card?

Bo watches as his Fish & Game info is embossed onto the yellow fish ticket and takes his copy. To scan a rough tally of weights amounting to almost 2800 pounds, Which even if you figure in the lower-priced smalls and #2s and end up a little less than I figured, still pretty good I guess. But more theoretical at this point than the work I still have to do.

—Hey Dave can I stay at the dock and wash

down if I slide back clear of the hoist?

—Bo. You're the last boat, it's midnight, I'm going home as soon as I help you get the last of your ice off. You can stay here and be a scrub-obsessed fanatic till eight in the fuckin' morning and it won't bother anyone.

The ice finally gone, a weary Bo clambers back down the ladder with brush sudsy pail and the plant's high volume hose to expunge blood and gurry. And root out three errant hearts and half a gill set from below a floorboard hatch. You terrorist organs lurking down here with intent to clog my bilge pump, out with you into the black harbor to sink and feed some bottom-scuttling crab. Jesus I am tired. I am so tired I care no thing that it's now too late to get a drink. I am so tired I wonder if I can climb out of this fish hold or shall I just lie down and make my bed here. I think not. I think I will climb this ladder and then the one up to the dock and then the stairs to the second floor where in the fishermen's shower room I may attain a next-to-godly state.

Or at least a less itchy one.

* * *

Scrubbed and mellowed to near inertia, Bo summons enough energy to distribute fenders and extra mooring lines and casts off. To motor at low idle toward Thompson along the quiet channel. Dim light in cabins of boats tied to the outer floats, plotters still turned on, or late night video junkies…weaving down the fairways here's my slip all's left is to glide in and cleat these lines and I am finally finished.

Or will be once I make the five minute drive to Voroni street and a soft bed with clean sheets to wake up in. Where'd I put the key.

Twenty minutes later, Bo leaning in utter fatigue against someone's Range Rover having made two futile circuits of the parking lot. Where the fuck is my fucking truck I can't have left it somewhere else. Although I try to remain a curious inhabitant of this universe I am not an epic seeker, I gladly leave the grail to Ulysses the search for the honest soul to Diogenes the grand unified theory to quarkers and string theorists, all I want is to not expire from exhaustion here in this cold unfeeling landscape of unfamiliar bumpers and alloy wheels. Wait over there is that my distinctive windshield wiper it is by God I am found.

Shedding shoes on the porch, Bo lets himself in quietly latching the door and padding softly down the carpeted hallway.

—ReeYOW

God damn cats so full of themselves can't conceive someone might fail to detour around them even when they're invisible in the dark.

—Is that you Bo?

—Mostly Homer but me too sort of.

—How was your trip?

—Not too bad…yeah, not bad at all.

—That's good.

—Yeah…well I'm dead beat I'm gonna turn in if I can find my bed see you tomorrow.

Closing the door against cat intrusion, Bo strips and slides happily beneath the covers to drop into deep seamless sleep and later at some point to a vivid dream, soft pressure of warm thighs on his, hands in fur covered mittens caressing and stroking him to taut yearning met by full lips descending sensuously oh God I am engulfed in bliss…

Waking midmorning in a state of pure satisfaction. Which might not last and therefore should be savored by lying here as long as possible—okay now I'm going to get up because it's been forever since that last can of Dinty Moore. In the kitchen a glass of orange juice on the table and a note

—I'm off to my honest toil have a byootiful day XX K

Symbolic kisses…fresh oj…wait…maybe that wasn't a dream?

CHAPTER 4

Outside, an ominously dark sky, darker still to the west with Mt. Edgecumbe entirely obscured, Verstovia at the town's back visible only on its lower slopes. Bo walking downhill to the Lincoln to stretch legs after two days' confinement on his 44' X 12' platform. Al occupying the first booth with a couple of young guys, green prospective crew from the look of the elementary seine layout sketched on a placemat.

—Hey Bo. Heard you licked 'em at Salisbury. Congratulations.

Jesus news travels fast in this town.

—Thanks Al. So that's how seining works, huh. What's with the line with all the floats on it, do you cinch it around the skiff so it can't get in the way when you're fishing?

—That's pretty lame Bo. Hey there's your friend Arguello at the counter. I bet he'd appreciate your thoughts even more than we do.

Bo slips in next to a lean form scowling at a compacted Watchdog Monday edition. Ashtray cigarettes and matches close at hand despite the town's new ordinance against inside smoking. Looking up and glancing to his left.

—Hey Wade.

—Hey. Asshole.

—Same to you then. How come you always fold your paper up like a bus commuter? Trying not to take up too much space is, like, diametrically opposite to how I see your personality.

Wade's gaze rising, intense blue eyes.

—Long as you've come over here to put your head in the lion's mouth, how about if I skunk you?

—Welcome to try.

Bo retrieving from behind the counter deck of cards, worn spruce cribbage board and a brown plastic pill bottle from which he selects four purplish-white sea urchin spines.

Wade shuffling, cutting the low card and dealing.

—You know it's going to rain? Says the Watchdog. One of those myopic reporters must have finally looked outside. And who's the nimrod that does this Xword puzzle? Today's all about WNBA teams. Does anybody give a shit about the WNBA?

—Well, sure...I mean, the level of play isn't up to the mens' but the games can be pretty good…Trish! Can I have a short stack of blueberries? And a coffee? And water? And a smile?

—Sure Bo. Decaf smile okay? Been a long morning…I hear you did real well on the opening I'm happy for you.

Wade pairing Bo's six.

—Asshole. Twelve for two.

Bo playing a third six.

—Eighteen for six points.

—Double asshole.

Bo losing the early lead and trailing through two streets until his pancakes arrive and they set the game aside.

—You don't eat breakfast?

—The civilized man recognizes breakfast as a meal to be consumed ante meridian rather than at a quarter to fuckin' lunch, and has enjoyed his many hours earlier. Speaking of late awakenings, how is the lovely Karen?

Bo busying himself in dumping most of a syrup pitcher on his two pancakes. Does the grapevine know everything?

—Not sure—haven't seen her in a few days (not strictly a lie).

—You're lucky I'm not a dentist, I'd have to strongly advise against such sugar excess. She is, sure, a gem of a woman, you should get serious.

—I'm even luckier you're not a life coach. She's great, I'm glad we're friends. Why don't you deal.

Okay here you are. I'm getting a distinct odor of *mephitis mephitis* here...these two for the crib and the cut if you please...that'll do. Did you really catch 100 the first day?

—God what a load of squat in these cards. No that was the second day. I had 500 the first.

Card on card Bo losing steadily, finishing the hand 20 away from the skunk line on third street plus 15 more to catch up to where Wade is positioned to go out.

—Okay how many really.

—Really want to know.

—Yeah.

—One ninety three. Little over half the first day.

—Jesus, Jesus. And you gave no thought to calling your friend. Damn I'm going to have to give you a setup in the crib. I hate to do it but I can't break up this hand.

—Yeah right, I'm sure you had the radio turned way up listening for my call when you were up to your ass in fish at the Cape the first morning. Sheeit, what friend didn't call me Friday to make sure I knew about the opening, I almost missed the whole thing! How's this for a cut.

— I think it'll help you more'n me. Well, I tried, check your inbox from nine Friday night, you weren't picking up.

—Yeah, I was out…celebrating…or something… at the Quixote Club. How many'd you get anyway? I don't think you're gonna skunk me.

—Eighty-five. Fifty by nine the first morning, 70 by dark and a pissant 15 the whole next day. Here I've got fifteen four and the double run of four for fourteen—two short of going out. No skunk if you say then but I'll settle for a decisive victory…why are you grinning like that?

—Number one you being all broken up about only getting 70 kings in a day…two, my hand which as you see is fifteen six and a triple run for 21 and then this crib which I put two fives in, to go with the jack five you gave me and the one you cut, look Wade it's the 29 hand is it not a thing of beauty? I'm out.

Arguello staring goggle eyed for a moment

—Fuck this I've got better things to do I'm out of here.

Grabbing his Camels and wheeling away.

That was a beautiful win, too bad he had to get so prickly. But it's not the cribbage, it's the fish he's sore about. Just like I'd be if he'd doubled me, probably. Ah well he'll get over it.

Checking out the abandoned, mostly completed Xword. Look at this he's got it all filled in except the WNBA teams, deliberately left them out. What a misogynist. What's this about rain. 'A deep 985 millibar low to cross the coast this afternoon. Southeast winds to 50 knots. Rain heavy at times.' Glad I'm not going anywhere. Although come to think of it, I better go hit the fuel dock before the wind comes up.

Laying a bill on the table, Bo pushing out the door

—Bo!

That is my name…

—Bo!

Squinting nonplussed, it's a female person, medium height, a face far from striking though pleasant enough, strangely distracting green eyes—who?

—Bo! I'm so glad! I had no idea how to get hold of you, and you were so nice I really thought we might get to know each other—

Bo staring now, striving for clues… unsuccessfully…his gaze falling—wait—is that not the same chest that abruptly bounced up and out the door of the Quixote, but—what happened to the rest of the lanky ideal dazzling beauty?

—Oh, yeah, how are you —

—I'm good you know I was just thinking maybe we could have dinner together or lunch you know would today work? Or maybe tomorrow…

—Uh, sure that's an idea but look I've got to keep moving here …

—Oh. Well here let me give you my number do you have anything to write on?

Bo finding a Texaco receipt in back pocket and replacing it newly inscribed after an awkward goodbye. Driving the back way past Swan Lake to avoid thronging tourists, the sky darkening and the first rain falling, bladeless passenger side wiper arm articulated forward off the glass keeping time in a small arc. I should stop in here at NAPA and replace that. But it can wait the wind'll be coming up soon.

Out in the channel, rain beginning to fall in curtains, pocking a surface that's strangely unruffled by any breeze. But it'll be here soon enough. Damn! Two boats already tied up at the Texaco float, now I'll have to drift around waiting for a spot. Shit oh dear it's the Breeze, and another of his clique that seem to do everything together, if the rest are lurking around here I can forget about getting fueled today. Can't see anyone, though—hey look it's my lucky day, that one's casting off his lines, it's the Pastor.

Bo taking a smooth curve to the dock, port side to and bow angled in so when he reverses it sucks the stern close and he can step off and cleat lines left coiled over the gunnels. Where's the man, I'm going to need this meter reset, here he comes.

—Hi Jack. Looks like we all waited till it started raining to fuel up.

—Nah, there was plenty of you earlier too. Some rumor there's going to be another opening next week.

—Really? That'd be weird. I'll start with the starboard tank.

Bo hauling the thick hose under the handrail and across the fish hold as Jack unspools. Pipewrenching the cap off the fill and lowering the nozzle, wedge jammed under the lever so he can go below and monitor the sight tube. Peaceful down here in the engine room, just the steady sound of flowing diesel and a few ticks from the cooling Cummins. All the time I've spent squatting like this over the last six years. Might almost be worth making a little fold-down seat, get another two weeks out of my knees when I'm 80. Ha, lucky if I get past 60. There goes the bubble disappearing up into the fitting. Twenty more gallons by the time I get back on deck.

On the dock, a green-coated and -hatted figure hauling a blue five gallon jug of Delo lube oil down the dock. Bo's hackles rising. This Mack on the Breeze may have some unobservable qualities which balance his scorched earth approach to trolling.

Unlikely, though, since he's never been known to be other than an asshole on the drag, assuming the right of way no matter which direction he's going.

Bo topping off and screwing the pipe cap back on before hauling hose to port and starting again. No need to go below with this tank which reliably expands with a hollow clank at fifteen gallons short of full. Rain really coming down now, I'd better lean over and keep it from dribbling into the tank.

The front seriously hitting by the time Bo settles the bill and casts off, gusts catching the tall poles and heeling the Walter over to starboard as he motors toward the marina entrance. Go ahead, kick me around, fitting accompaniment to sad memories… ...Mariella….

CHAPTER 5

Just outside the inner breakwater, the phone in Bo's pocket sounding the first bar of Beethoven's ninth. Who is that distracting me just when it gets tricky, I'll circle around here. Arguello, it says.

—Hey Wade.

—Where are you? We should go visit the Quixote.

—Excellent idea but I'm busy driving around in the rain. I'll be tied up in five minutes. Where are you?

—On the boat. I'll walk over and watch you crash into stuff.

Bo plotting as he approaches F dock. This wind will shove me right into the Audrey if I come in with it on the stern, I'll have to back down past the slip and then come back and curve in to the left. Here we are, a little back and forth to get the bow up into the wind, then a bunch of reverse down the fairway, okay now goose her upwind and a hard left turn...ease in till we nudge the dock and then with the bow pushing against the boards, left rudder'll bring the stern in and there's good old Wade tying me off.

—Hey you're all wet I don't know if I should let you in here you'll drip.

Arguello removing oilskin jacket and shaking it vigorously, sizzle of drops hitting the oil stove across from the settee.

—There now I won't. What's in this cupboard, ha, a partial bottle of Canadian Mist. I suggest a game of cribbage before we pay our visit to the Don. Loser buys dinner?

—That's fine. I'm going to make a cup of cocoa for my whiskey, need to warm up. You too?

—Sounds good.

—Okay, here's the cards, you want to shuffle. Kettle's not quite ready, I'll just move it onto the hot spot. Jack says there might be another opening next week, you heard that?

—Yeah, everyone's blabbing it up, but Laurie at Fish and Game says she hasn't heard anything. Christ, I hope it's just a rumor, I've got plenty of boat work before the main opening which I trust you're aware is only a week and a half away. Gotta lay my poles down, stupid springs are about rusted through. I don't see why someone doesn't make them out of stainless.

—I'm sure you could find some, you want to spend five times what the galvanized ones cost—two springs per line, three lines per pole, you do the whole rig and some spares, you've spent enough to buy, what, half a ticket to Cabo….

—Who the fuck wants to go to Cabo?

— I'm just saying, all that glitters is not eternal,

stainless gets brittle, you know—

—Bullshit artificial moneysucking tourist sump, I can't believe you'd want to spend time down there, crowds of spring break drunks and puffed up sportsfishermen slobbering to torture a sailfish before making a fake fiberglass model of it to hang on the wall—

—Easy, easy, I was just talking about going somewhere warm in the winter—

—Plastering hotels all over those beautiful beaches and filling the harbor with million dollar sport boats driving the moorage cost past outrageous.

—I'm sorry already, I didn't know your family was displaced from their bucolic life there, humbly raising a few cows and pigs until evil capitalist developers put the boot down on their idyllic scene.

—My family's from Oregon as I'm sure you know but we visited Cabo when I was a kid and I can tell you it sucks now.

—I suppose if you were from Manhattan you'd be crying about how there's no beach to dig clams on any more.

—New York at least got some world class culture along with the density, what's Cabo got, grim hotel discos on the beach with wet t-shirt contests?

—You're all of a sudden against wet t-shirts?

—I'm for no-shirt contests. Why screw around?

—Yeah, well. Here's your whisco, you going to cut for deal or what?

Cabin lamps on against the dark as black storm

clouds overpower the declining sun, gale driven rain spattering the starboard windows, creak of straining lines when heavy gusts buffet the boat. Small pool of warm friendly light spilling onto the dock, a tiny gleam in the immensity of the frontal system pounding the Baranof shore.

Stuttering progress of pegs up and down the cherrywood board and a falling level of amber liquid. On fourth street of the second game, Wade squeaking out by making a run during the play. Upending the bottle to harvest a few remaining drops.

—I'm fucking starving. Let's get gone, I've got a feeling you're not cooking tonight.

—Wouldn't mind if I had any food on board…wait, there's one more big can of Dinty Moore—

—We were talking about food. You the driver?

—Sure.

Out Sawmill Creek Road past the last houses, spruce branches flailing wildly in the wind. Lights on high beam boring a short hole ahead in the torrent-filled dark. Bo shifting uncomfortably behind the wheel.

—Hope they've got the heater up high, pants got totally soaked just getting to the truck. LA's in a five year drought, sucking so much water out of the Sacramento the salmon can't get upstream and we've got way more water than we need.

—That's why the Russians built Swan Lake here, you know.

—What?

—Dammed it in thinking they'd let it freeze, cut ice chunks out and ship it south. I don't know how much they followed through. But there's a thought for your next business venture.

—Thanks. Here we are, I'm going to run for it. Ready?

—I'm not running anywhere. Find me a good seat.

The Quixote mostly vacant on this Monday evening. Bo choosing a table directly below a heat vent near the bar, draping streaming slicker over chair back as Wade ambles up. Bartender appearing at the same time, dealing coasters, nervously watching as Arguello lays Camels and lighter on the table.

—Fellas. You want to order some food, or just drinks?

—Hey Herman. I'll have this special, the Southwest Grilled Fowl Grinder with fries. Canadian on the rocks.

—Gimme the High Density Lipid Burger. Also fries. Same to drink.

—You got it. You make it through the scuffle and get home okay the other night, Bo?

—No problems. That was weird though huh, guys fighting about pronunciation.

— Should've been here the next night. This halibut fisherman from Kodiak starts going off about how ignorant everyone in Southeast is cause they pronounce that bay up past Cape Spencer, Astrolabe is it? like 'wallaby.' Which since it's like a British sextant or something, it should rhyme with babe. The locals got in his face and the guy's crew ran over from the pool table and went grizzly before I could do anything—broke two cue sticks, somebody got a bad gash on his temple and we had to call the aid car. Thought sure the police would show up and hassle me but apparently there was an even bigger fight at the Pioneer.

—Lucky you.

—Yeah. I'll go get started on these orders.

Wade, after a moment's thought, theorizing.

—Know what I think? I think Herman's setting the Quixote up to bring in the Lesbian crowd.

—What? What crowd…what the hell are you talking about?

—Think about it, this pattern of arguments. You got to admit, he seems to be attracting some cunning linguists.

Bo staring blankly for a minute…

—Jesus, that's sick. You're sick! Ah, here's our whiskey just in time. Here's to a respite from the lowest form of humor.

—Okay, cheers. But look, even if that guy was one of these primitive longliners that drop dead bait down with anchors to lure bizarre disgusting bottom feeding creatures into attaching themselves to his line with their lips, so he can haul them up and rip the hook out with a crucifier—even so, you have to admit he had a point. Half the time we don't know what we're saying around here.

—You're implying, half the time we do?

—Like that island inside Cross Sound, got a name of obviously French origin but everyone calls it 'Lemisher'.

—I don't get in there much, makes me claustrophobic to fish where you can't see the ocean.

—Anyway it's spelled 'Lemesurier'. Lehmuhzooreeay.

—Lemoo… Lemizzery—fuck it. Lemisher's easier. Why make extra work for yourself? It's like that channel down by Dixon Entrance, that Spanish one with all the syllables, nobody even tries it, they just say 'the channel south of Ketchikan.' Oh boy here's our food. Another Canadian, Herman?

Conversation ebbing, giving way to sounds of devourment. Resuming during the judicious selection of last remaining French fries.

—Man! Those onions bite back, don't they? Hope you don't have plans for an intimate engagement later with a member of the fairer sex.

—To be sure, I should check my appointment book, but I don't believe so. Anyway, you never know when you might find a woman whose appreciation of the noble bulb takes in all its wide delivery of taste sensations.

—Can't really imagine anyone like that—well, there's Herman's cook….

—She's good, isn't she? Maybe she wants to go fishing.

—Doubt if he'd go for that, it's his wife, he met online last year. Was cooking at some fancy hotel in

Pusan. I'm surprised you didn't order her black cod in ginger and lime sauce considering I'm buying.

—Shit! I forgot.

—So how are you and Alsea getting along, okay?

—It gets a little close, dark winter in Fairbanks and all, she complains I yell too much. We'll see how the fishing goes, nothing like being on a small boat to catalyze things.

Flow interrupted by a looming presence approaching unsteadily from the bar. Beefy, mid twenties, shaved head and an iron cross tattoo visible on left side of neck over sleeveless sweatshirt. Glaring at Arguello.

—It's illegal to smoke in here. And I heard what you were sayin about longliners. You should put those fuckin cigarettes away and you should keep your fuckin mouth shut.

Bo groaning.

—Oh shit here we go.

Wade replying reasonably.

—I believe you are laboring under a misconception, I am not in fact smoking and so there is no problem is there.

—Everybody else had to quit smoking in here and you're nobody special so put em away.

Wade rising, pushing his chair back.

—I believe everyone is special on this green earth, even you. So I will take the time to explain this again. I am not smoking therefore you have no complaint.

—What do you got them there for then.

—That's my business.

—That's bullshit is what it is, you got em, you're gonna smoke em, get rid of em or I will.

—Look here. We are both wearing boots, right? Now I wanted to, I could use one to dislocate your kneecap. You might be able to do the same thing. But that doesn't give anybody the right to tell me or you to go barefoot. So forget about my smokes, get out of my face, and GO SIT THE FUCK DOWN.

Delivered at increasing volume, the last at full roar. Other patrons staring. Herman hurrying out from behind the bar, the complainant grabbing the cigarettes and with pack fisted grazing Wade's cheek before aiming a vicious kick at his groin but with some delay in windup, Wade able to step back and give the heavy booted foot a lift toward the ceiling toppling its belligerent owner backward to knock head on stained carpet. Groggily getting back to hands and knees.

—What the fuck's

Herman glaring as he grabs an arm and begins hauling

—Goddammit Wade what is with you and your stupid Camel game.

—happening—

—You think you gotta teach everyone a lesson?

—anyway I run into something?

Herman providing guide service back toward the bar.

—Yeah you ran into something all right, some guy that's carrying around both the rock AND the hard place.

—Isn't that guy a deckhand on the Breeze?

—Yeah. Prerequisite for employment with Mack's crowd: must be certified asshole.

—True that, but...you know, it could be true you got some anger management issues.

—Bullshit. I'm doing a perfectly fine job managing my anger. I should let it get all knotted up inside and make me sick?

—I dunno what you should do. Sometimes I wonder if knocking all these fish in the head helps a guy work things out, or just makes him more hostile.

—Probably both.

—Anyway, what's with talking shit about longliners, like you don't fish Chatham black cod yourself?

—Yeah well it's still an uncivilized way to catch fish compared to trolling.

The recent contretemps dampening the conversation. Two more whiskey rounds and an attempt to revive with dessert inspiring Arguello to deliver himself of a brief but fervent rant about the failure of America to institute a national health care plan. The plain superiority of the Canadian and European systems. The appalling Congressional combination of ignorance and industry bribes, finally passing a pale ghost of what should have been. Tapering off, face taking on a glazed look.

Bo tripping to the head to consider a thread among the banal obscenities scrawled above the urinal.

—Ahmedinejad blows goats

—Netanyahu blows Palestinian sheep

—Cheney blew everything in sight

—Support the troops you assholes

Urine smell strangely strengthening, the room making an abrupt 90-degree lurch to the right. Oh shit the whirlies. Quick find water. Bo zipping up to weave back to the table and glug down both glasses left with the dinner and one and a half more from nearby table. The centrifugal effect slowing. Resuming seat and looking across at Wade, passed out face down in plate of cherry pie. Shit. Time to wrap this up. Attempt at revival, shaking arm.

—Damn. Hey Arguello! Wake up! Thass no way to treat a lady. Come on, man, HEY! Wake the fuck up!

—rrrrrrrrg. Leggo me. Ize having really good dream.

—Come on come on let's get goin.

Bo hauling friend close to vertical and in odd mutually supportive combination slaloming past the bar and out into parking lot. And into even denser rainfall. Whose marginal sobering effect helps Bo get Wade situated in passenger seat and himself behind the wheel. Stalling the truck twice before nosing out to road verge. Which way. Town is west, rain is blowing from right so west may be is right I'll try right.

Proceeding with extreme caution. Wade again asleep, head against window. Can't hardly see shit but I think I recognize these curves. Up to the top of this rise and the trail down to where Trish lives, solace there, forget that. Down the backside of the hill raining even harder now center line a blur Jesus Christ it's like a whiteout I better take it out of gear and coast slowly down, light touch on the brake pedal. Windshield full of rain even with wiper on high speed. I guess I'm still on the road anyway, just keep easing on down.

Time attenuating. Hands tight on wheel, mind fully in storm zone. This is one long hill. Presently from the passenger's seat a Spanish inflected declaration.

—Revillagigedo.

—What?

—Channel by Keshikan.

Wade peering out. Lowering window to poke head out into storm. Withdrawing, soaked, dripping from nose and chin.

—Wassup. Why not moving.

—Huh? Gotta go slow. Can see shit.

—You're parked.

—Huh?

Bo rolling down his own window, leaning out to be lashed by rain and gust. And contemplate a stationary yellow dash on the spattered pavement.

Re-rolling window. Consider this for a moment.

—Okay. I guess I'n go a little fasser.

Shifting back into gear and resuming progress. This'll work, check out side window now and then keep the centerline from sneaking off into the dark. There we go. Good ole yellow line.

Presently a red glow off to the right. Wass? Oh,

stop sign. Must be Lake Street. Turn right. Rain a little lighter here in lee of town hill, I'n kina sce the shoulder. Take these curves nice and slow. Another glow, light at Katlian. Green very lucky color, cruise on through left turn and downslope a block to bump into the Thompson lot and park skewed across three spaces.

—Hey. We got here. Wanna hang till you're good make it down the dock, 'scool. Don fall in.

No response. Bo exiting to slog along sidewalk past yellow glow of the cold storage building's security light, finding the path entrance off to the left. A loose rock halfway up, Bo swaying, grabbing a salmonberry to keep from toppling backwards.

—Ow fuck thorns. But here we are. Good ole Olds mole—wait better haul pants down agains the spenders and offload a bunch a that water I chugged ahhh. How bout that you nine hunner millbar low my deluge jus as strong as—oop better turn siways I think I may be piss on feet. 'K now. Get in shelter how the hell the door hannel works. Button on which end. There we go yeah. Nice thing bout iss hotel don't hafta take off rain gear get in bed. Jus lie here in the dry an…

Police Response Unwarranted, Says Local Dog Owner

By Myra Wooley

Details are only now emerging as to the police action Sunday night in the 1400 block of Burdock Street, when officers responded to a disturbance of the peace call.

Residents claim that they were awakened without cause at three in the morning, and that police used a heavy handed threatening tone.

"Posy did absolutely nothing wrong," said Rita Brafly, who lives at the address the police were called to. "This is all because Hans Kuchen next door can't sleep on account of his wife's little dalliance with---well, that's all I'll say about that."

Posy is the adorable half Husky, half Samoyed who lives with the Braflys. She is a friendly, affectionate pet, as this reporter discovered during the course of an exhaustive investigation into the circumstances. It is just hard to believe she could offend anyone.

But some people may be inordinately sensitive.

"Two or three times a week that dog is barking very loud in the middle of the night, and I finally got tired of it waking me up and called the police," stated Mr. Kuchen irritably when interviewed by a reporter.

"Well she certainly does not bark as you can see," responded Mrs. Brafly. "Maybe a little yip now and then if a squirrel or a porcupine trespasses on our property. But she has the sweetest personality,

don't you think"

Posy's appearance is nothing like what you might expect from a mean Disturber of the Peace, what with her pink-tongued smile and eagerness to roll over for tummy rubs. But maybe some people just don't like dogs.

"That dog is a psychopath," insisted Kuchen. "The neighborhood is nice and quiet at night, and then it starts barking inside the house, and they put it outside, and it goes on barking at nothing, for hours. What's it defending us from, mice?"

"Look at her coat, how clean and shiny it is," Rita pointed out. "Does she look like someone who would get all rabid and slobbery about a mouse, or anything? Of course not."

Police Chief Denny Chaw said that although his Department warned the Braflys to comply with the Noise Ordinance, they cannot take any direct action unless they witness a violation taking place. However, if two successive complaints are made, they may take an animal into custody, he said, while being interviewed.

Those in our town who appreciate pets may conclude that to prevent a grouchy neighbor from causing an innocent animal to be locked up, they should begin attending Borough meetings to get their representatives to change this law to be more fair to our animal friends.

□

CHAPTER 6

Bo setting aside the Watchdog upon arrival of breakfast. Dungeness crab omelet which will hopefully scavenge the demons at play in my skull. I believe this is some familiar person easing into the stool next door.

—Hey Bo.

—Hey Gary. What is.

—Is not much. How's with you?

— I pain, therefore I am. Head hurts big time.

—Still trying to exorcise your demons with alcohol overdose, huh? How's it going with that?

—Know what? I'm not quite ready for an encounter therapy session. How about if we postpone till after breakfast.

—Oh fine fine I'll mute my friendly concern. How about the opener coming up, what are you thinking?

—What, they are really going to have another insider before the first?

—Naw, that was just some rumor Gertie Rick started. He's got this idea if you make enough buzz about something it'll happen. But no, I'm talking about July. You think Salisbury'll go off again?

—Oh, yeah, no question. I personally asked those fish to hang out for two weeks till I came back. But (glancing around melodramatically) we shouldn't talk it up. Don't want the secret to get out, right?

— Okay, I know, unlikely there'd be another big hit like you had. But I just thought you might've seen some sign?

—You know Gary if we hadn't fished together as long as we have, I'd think you were some kind of groupie trying to bask in the glow of my recent success.

—Yeah well. You are kinda the bomb around the fleet right now. I'm just glad I can say, I knew you when you were a regular guy. Before you had Kim Kardashian's cell number.

— I'll try to remember my roots. Anyway, I don't know where I'm gonna start out. Probably go farther west, like usual.

—That's what I'm thinking, check some spots on the way, wind up on the Fairweather Grounds if nothing shows.

—Yeah. Well, let's get together with Wade and figure out a radio channel before we go, we can regroup our big three-boat fleet.

—Sounds good. I gotta split, I'm hauling out Friday and got to buy zincs and paint and stuff. Hey, it's supposed to clear up tomorrow, a few of us are going up Harbor Mountain, have a little cookout, want to come?

—Lessee…I have to pick my deckhand up at the airport around ten thirty…but we'd be back by then, right?

—Definitely, folks have to work in the morning.

—Okay, that'd be great…I'll be on the boat. Let me know when you're taking off?

—Will do. See ya.

Attention returned to breakfast, the serious kid who replaces Trish Monday to Wednesday refilling coffee, Bo recovering enough to consider the Watchdog crossword puzzle. Let's see, one across six letters, trim or neaten (up), who knows but P might be the second letter because two down, four letters for yearn could be pine…one down nine letters, German canine breed, Schnauzer, right? Which means one across could be…spruce? Yeah, spruce, pine, I'm seeing the pattern here…what's this five down, six letters starting with C meaning hymen…huh? Wait a second that can't be

—I didn't know you were one of those *intellectuals*, Bo.

The term pronounced as if synonymous with syphilitics, the speaker looming up to occupy 150 percent and then some of the next stool.

—Oh, hi Rick. You don't like puzzles?

—I guess they're okay, long as you don't have something honest to occupy yourself with. But at least you know how to catch fish unlike these Fish and Game bean counters, which they can't tell a salmon from a sperm whale far as I can tell. You gonna try Salisbury again this next opening? Pretty impressive show you put on.

This is, like, *déjà vu* plus 50 percent.

—I don't know. Who can say what'll happen in two weeks?

—Naw, I don't mean July. The inside opening, they're gonna announce for next week.

—Come on. There's never been a hatchery opening that close to the regular season. What makes you think they'll start now?

—Just because Fish and Game's been running things doesn't mean they know squat. Gimme a break—these *biologists*, they sit in a classroom for four years, they're experts on fishing? Fishery schools want to get real, they should put their campus fifty miles up the darn Stikine River and make their *intellectuals* sit on the bank every day to see the fish coming back to spawn. Then they might learn something.

— I guess that's one way to look at it…so you really think if enough people say there's going to be an opening, they'll have an opening?

—Yeah, if it's based on on-the-grounds input. What are they going on as it is? They stare into their computers at a bunch of random numbers and make something up. They gotta be suffering from disconnect, operating like that, so if we give them something real to go on, they'll eat it up, eat it up like, what, like that regular salad stuff they're always talking up on the cooking channel, which I tried it once and it didn't help the constipation at all, another yuppie scam.

—uhh...arugula, you mean?

—Whatever, it doesn't work. But what will work is if they get some real data, from real fishermen. Not that they'll be smart enough to see the advantage right away. I tried to help out, applied to have National Marine Fisheries put an observer on my boat and they said no.

—You actually wanted somebody looking over your shoulder out there?

—Sure I did. Hey, I'll play by the rules till we change them. And what's the best way to do that? Show 'em! Get one of them out there away from their twitter and their facebook, put 'em on deck during a bite so they can see how many fish there are. But they turned me down, said I had to have a flush toilet on board. How lame is that? Five gallon bucket qualifies as a holding tank for the Coast Guard, but it's not good enough for a NMFS kid.

—I used to use a bucket, my first boat. Wasn't so bad, the dent the edge made around your butt always went away after five or ten minutes.

—I got a varnished plywood seat I made, fits on top—it's plenty comfy. But screw the observer program, I got other avenues. Anyway, I better go get back to Gertie, we've got plenty to do before it opens again, I'm thinking it'll be next Tuesday. Maybe you'll have a chance to repeat your big Salisbury slam there, fish assassin.

Bo forking up the last omelet fragments. Next Tuesday he thinks. Loony as a Maine lagoon. Not a bad head though. Appreciated my accomplishment.

Kind of interesting, being a celebrity like this. I wonder how far it'll go. I suppose WKAT might want to interview me…story could get picked up at the national level…maybe some NPR producer'll hear it and get excited. Sure, I could see a reality show with me out there on the Walter, that'd have some strong appeal. Wow. This thing could really snowball. I wonder who'll be the next admirer.

Take a covert glance around, see who might be approaching. Hm. Place is pretty deserted. Well, I might as well go get to work too.

—Bo!

Ha! Just as I reach the door, another devotee. Guess I can be gracious, spare some time—

—Bo! Aren't you gonna pay your bill?

CHAPTER 7

The channel calm as Bo motors south past the fish plant. Small crowd of gulls circling around an offloading longliner, diving on bits of gurry that a hidden shoveler is pitching out of the hold with bloody used ice. The sullen persistent rain that had prevailed on Bo's trek from bed to breakfast turned now to drizzle. Slight lightening in the sky to the southwest. Maybe it will get nice tomorrow, that'd be okay, I can handle a barbecue on the mountain. There's the pole dock sticking out just past the Coast Guard base…shit, there's already someone there, damn it. Hold on—it's the Sobrino. Guess Wade recovered early.

Bo slowing, fixing fenders to starboard side, Arguello visible hunched over end of lowered starboard pole oblivious of approach, possibly due to vast volume of music emitting from open doors of the steel troller's wheelhouse. Strings behind a reedy solo filling the surrounding acre of water and beach with some haunting melody. Bo securing lines, climbing over bulwarks and onto the dock.

—Wade!

—Wade!...*HEY WADE!*

Arguello finally looking up. Fluttering hand in Bo's direction.

—Silence there! Hang on. This is the last selection, over in a minute.

Bo perching on the Sobrino's rail, craning up at the port pole. New tag lines, good, he's done with that side, I'll be able to move in when he finishes the other—what is this music? The woodwind voice rising through a series of major arpeggios, pensively tapering off before swooping back down to join the strings in a thrumming finish. Arguello clambering over the lowered pole's stays, cordless drill in hand, vice grips and other tools sticking out of pockets in brown coveralls. "Chuck" embroidered in red on breast pocket.

—What is that instrument?

—That is the masterful Lajos Lensces on oboe, playing a piece by Mozart who I suppose you are aware was no slouch himself.

—Sure…hey, how is it that the most beautiful music has such a strong sorrowful feel?

—Life itself is sad, my friend. Like flying fish we burst on the scene to skitter over succeeding wavetops, only too soon to run out of momentum and sink back into the universal sea.

—Yeah. To be eaten by something bigger. Like a ratfish.

—Possibly. But no need to smite your brow in dismay. After dispersing once again into the whole, many of our constituent parts may rejoin and we'll be reborn in a different form.

—Like, a baby ratfish.

—Well. It's apparent your philosophical development has been stunted, likely by some combination of television and popular culture, so we may as well turn to the mundane. I see you've attached your boat to mine, is there some intention there?

—Let's see, there must've been…what was it…providing protective coloration to foil any parole officers or ex-wives who might be looking for you? That's a good possibility, given my generous nature. Either that, or I'm patiently waiting for you to get the fuck off the dock so I can lower my own poles.

—Let's presume the latter, despite your gratuitously rude and blunt verbiage. Toward that end, if you would go aft and hold out those short lines from the fairleads, I could connect the tag lines now and avoid them snarling when I raise the pole.

Bo leaning out over the water between stern and dock, tight one-handed grip on overhead pipe frame extending out past the Sobrino's rail. Proffering the lines' looped ends for Wade to snap the longer wires from the pole tips to. The pipe then offering a handy purchase from which to do a pull-up.

—This is one fancy aluminum hayrack. I bet you could've flown to Cabo three or four times for what it cost. You going to rig all six lines now, be ready to start out west of Spencer?

—No, I'll just set up four for now, that's all we'll

be able to use on the inside opening next week.

Bo staring.

—Next week. God damn. The mindset of Gertie Rick is infiltrating every sentient being in this town. Not to mention you. This is like some horror movie. What stage are you at, is it just that your mind's been erased, or can you infect others as well?

Wade extending clutched hands

—I am going…to bite…your neck

Bo cringing exaggeratedly and Wade relaxing.

—I'm just saying what everyone else was in the gear store this morning. Tuesday, I think it's supposed to be.

—How in the hell does he do this. Well, it's not gonna happen. I'll bet you dinner.

—Wouldn't want to rush into a bet like that, okay, you're on.

—Good. Now I know where at least one of my next meals is coming from. So about this pole of yours. Are you done? Are you done? Can I use the dock yet?

—Yeah, sure, I guess. Grab that tip line and help me haul her up into the crosstree.

* * *

Next afternoon, thin steam rising off the Walter's deck as a resurgent sun dries the storm's remnant damp spots. Below in the engine room, more steam in form of expletive blast as Bo contorts to distribute oil absorber pads on diesel spilled in bilge. The curse level gradually becoming milder. God damn it can't you pay attention to what you're doing. Or did you set this up by leaving the dirty fuel filter precariously perched. Maybe that was a subconscious attempt to choke off the self pitying recollection of Mariella that was creeping up God DAMN it why can't I let go. Always there just below the surface. Except when I'm on the way to a buzz. Or wholly into fishing like the other day. There's that other bottle I didn't tell Wade about the other night. But I should finish this…ahh, fuck.

Bo slumping against the starboard fuel tank to stare past the Cummins' valve cover at nothing…at everything….

PART TWO

Central Italy

CHAPTER 8

Bo giving up, soon after leaving the Fiumicino airport, trying to match speed on the autostrada with manifestations of German engineering that hurtle at 150 kph past his rented Fiat, it being clear from the tortured whining emitted by the little 1.6 liter engine that it will turn into a molten chunk of carbon long before he reaches Florence. The more relaxed pace allowing him to glance down at and memorize driving directions printed from the internet.

Only to find, on taking the Firenze Sud exit and crossing the Arno on the Ponte a Verlungo, that there are no street signs in the city. Continuing for a few kilometers on map memory and dumb luck before getting entirely lost. Now how do I find the hostel. Stopping to ask pedestrians for directions in Spanish salted with a few recently learned Italian phrases. Which combination must surely be understandable to these fellow Romantic language speakers. Receiving quizzical looks and advice given in clear English which, followed, only gets him further disoriented. Paranoia setting in. These good citizens revenging themselves for past despicable international policies of my country by purposely misdirecting the American tourist. One more try, jump out and intrude on this intently striding preoccupied woman—

—Per favore, donde esta Ostello San Gallo?

The reaction a finger pointed twenty feet away.

Well the sign's not all that large. Bo after considerable effort finding a free parking space and huffing his gear up a narrow stairway two floors to buzz into a small but clean reception and pay a dour young woman for a space in a four-bed room. Passing through the common area, a slim shorthaired blonde looking up from one of the two computer desks. Was there a hint of mischief in that smile. Maybe she'll still be there after I stow this gear. The only empty bunk an upper next to a window that will tonight hopefully admit some smaller fraction of the street racket that's coming in now.

She is still there, emailing by the looks of it, an inquisitive glance as Bo crosses to squat and browse a low bookcase wow it's been a long time since I saw a copy of Siddhartha.

—Buona sera, Americano

Bo looking up into deep blue eyes and another wide-lipped smile.

—Buona sera…Alemana?

—non e 'Alemana' in Italiano, piuttosto 'Tedesca'—but I am Swedish.

—Pues no hablo Italiano, sino Espanol.

—Well I would prefer to practice English than

Spanish.

—And I too prefer to practice a language other than my own.

—Maybe better that you speak Swedish, then.

Impasse solved by agreeing to alternate Spanish and English. And a subsequent agreement to seek dinner. Out in the twilit streets of the old city, traffic on the narrow sidewalk sometimes forcing them to walk single file, Bo happily noting when Ingrid goes first the way her hips move in tight jeans.

—Hey look, the street names are on the buildings!

—Of course! How old are you?

—Thirty-two, why?

—I guessed around that, and yet is your first time to Europe, how can that be?

—How could you tell—oh, I guess the streets are like this everywhere, huh. Well, I thought I'd wait until I was old, like maybe in my 70s, to come, because Europe is old and tired and preoccupied with the past. At least that's the impression I got from the slide shows of old cathedrals and ruined castles I had to sit through after my relatives went touring. I suppose that's a little stupid isn't it.

—No, *truly* stupid. Why are you now here.

—The hiking in the mountains to the north, friends tell me it is really good. And then I had a good season fishing last summer and could afford the trip. Maybe it was as much money as stupidity that kept me from coming sooner.

—So what (turning close, that smile again) do you think now, it is all old and backward?

—Still stuck before the Renaissance, if your street signs are any measure—

Ingrid giving him a hip check, Bo doing a quick sidestep to avoid a no parking sign. Dancing back to reach and take her hand

—But the people *on* the street are modern, and really attractive…at least one is...

Ingrid pressing into him, leaving her hand in his. Half a block farther, savory smells emerging from a door ajar beneath a modest sign Il Miraggio. Inside, a narrow L-shaped room, sounds of clinking utensils and low voices. This table at the back is open…pesce alla griglia, the polenta? How about this Chianti…the dishes pedestrian but good, the wine heightening the exchange of personal history, hopes for the future, growing eye contact your blue irises are such a pleasure to gaze into, grazie, non, no dessert we'll just have the bill.

Back through the dim lamplit streets on the way to the hostel, giving in to this spontaneous attraction, arms about each others' waists. Ingrid holding a serious consultation with the desk clerk before pulling Bo down the hall to her two-bed quarters as yet unshared.

—It is against the rules but she is kind.

The door closed, turning with expectant smile to face him and return a long embrace, Bo's joy at pulling her shirt up and watching the small breasts bounce as the fabric frees them to disappear under his hands, helping each other unbuckle, this is your lower bunk let's lie here and let our skins commune for a while, oh who has a safe there's one in my pants I have one here shall I, no I'll do it…okay, let's start over…oh you feel so good yes guide me in there just…so…good to feel this supple body moving slowly beneath me, so good to meet someone who finds fun in sex it feels so…oh so good….

Bo's drift into contented sleep interrupted

—You can't stay, I promised you'd go back to your room.

—Mmm…what? Really? Bezos no mas?

—Yes of course here is a kiss…now certainly, you have to go.

Bo pulling on enough clothing to be semipresentable, gathering the rest

—Okay, buenas noches, see you in the morning.

Climbing into his upper bunk, low snoring and an occasional muffled fart from his roommates and a periodic exceptionally loud reverberating roar as a truck motors through the canyon of the street outside, Bo's thoughts floating above the cacophony buoyed by anticipation of the next day with Ingrid—or days—or who knows—they could explore the city and then, maybe she'll want to come north and hike in the mountains or, she said her goal was to get south to, what was the town? South of Naples, anyway…that could be fun…it could all be fun, Ingrid, so nice to say Ingrid, Bo drifting off to a lingering vision of smiling blue eyes…

—Scheisse!

Bo jolted awake to look directly into different eyes, blue as well but grimacing, their curly-headed owner tenderly rubbing his scalp before leaving the room with a shaving kit. The other bunks already vacated, Bo removing watch from bedrail, Jesus it's 9, wow I slept well but time to get moving.

Dressing in anticipation, clean jeans and t-shirt, a quick head sluice in the washroom and out into the common…where there is no sign of Ingrid, nor in the kitchen, perhaps she's sleeping late too.

—Per favore, la signorina…que esta…por alla…como puedo…

—You want to see the Swedish girl. She left you this.

A folded note. *Good morning Americano. It was a big pleasure knowing you. It would be nice to have more time but I must go to meet my friend in Agropoli. Here is my telephone number at home so you can call me if you ever come to Stockholm. Con besos, Ingrid*

Bo sinking into a tired sofa, the note barely held between thumb and finger, if I relaxed my hand the least amount this paper would slip away just as she has. I was so over-committed, what a tragedy, the day now empty as a discarded cereal box. Would I feel better if I ate, if I found a cup of coffee, can I ever feel better? How could she do this. I guess it meant nothing, maybe the sophisticated European mentality takes sex for what it is and nothing more, maybe I am just a hick from Alaska, maybe I wish I had never come on this trip if it is just going to lead to emptiness.

Really. Would I rather last night never happened, of course not, let's be zen about this, it was a beautiful momentary attraction, and this is another moment, and there will be another coming along soon and perhaps it would be a better moment if I had some coffee to drink while it occurred.

Bo finding a half full overcooked pot in the kitchen along with an honor box to pay for rudimentary pastries, this culinary poverty will be suitable for my mood. Okay, let's buck up just a little and plot out on the back of this cruel thoughtless Viking's heart-plundering note how the rest of the day might go.

10:00 to 10:30: Feel sad and find a longer-term place to park the car.

10:30 to say 4:00: Feel sad and explore this ancient city in search of distraction...cathedrals?

4:00 to 6:30: Feel sad and return to hostel, use computer to plan hiking trip to the Dolomiti.

CHAPTER 9

Bo emerging from an underground garage near the railway station under a stubbornly gray October sky. Self-consciously unfolding a gaudy brochure picked up at the hostel. May as well face it, I am a tourist. So what do tourists do. Visit all these famous places, the Uffizi, Boboli Gardens, Ponte Vecchio, I can walk down here eight blocks and take a left and go another ten and I'll be well positioned to knock off all three.

Forty minutes later, Bo hung up in the Piazza della Signoria. I am supposed to wait in this long line to get in to the Uffizi Gallery but I hate waiting in line. Maybe I can absorb a sufficient quantity of art out here…for example, this fountain and its spurting bronze cherub… but what's this skinny fellow in tattered jacket rooting through a wire mesh trash bin nearby for. Ah, a styro cup, to hold in the cherub's stream and drink deep, recycling at its purest. Or maybe he is a performance artist.

The famous David across the square. Taking a pompous pose, with his oversize nudity and his curly hair and his complacent demeanor no doubt stemming from having a perfect body. Ignoring Neptune fifty feet to the west who, glaring at him, appears to be saying hey, punk, no doubt you're buff but look at me, old but still ready to roll, plus my fountain is clearly superior, with its fish, its naked attendants, the weird little squirting guys strangely tangled in the Neptunian legs…and these…stallions trying to leap out of the fountain?…Jesus the Latin imagination ran to strange lengths.

Farther along, recessed in the sides of the Gallery's courtyard, more statues of the city's early movers and shakers…Michaelangelo, Leonardo, Dante, I've heard of them…hey this guy's called Bocaccio, how cool that he named himself after a fish. But what's this statue out in the road, a woman in silver cat suit—oh, there's a donation box, it's a frozen mime.

I wonder if I could hold myself motionless like that. I'll just stand across the way and pose as, what, something natural—a tourist! Reading his touristic brochure, is what I will be. *Boboli became a model for all European Royal gardens including those in the Palace of Versailles*…is it okay for a frozen mime to move his eyes? I think I'm getting this…*besides the above mentioned Large Cave you should visit the Amphitheatre the Basin and the Island Tank originally meant for the cultivation of flowers and citrus fruit trees one of the garden's most evocative scenarios*…stop reading now…I am definitely in the zone now I wonder if it's okay to think or should I give up all thought, surrender to the Void…

ommmmmmmmmmmmmmmmmmmmmmmmmm
mmmmmmmmmmmmmmmmmmmmmmmmmmmm
mmmmmmmmmmmmmmmmmmmmmmmmmmmm
mmmmmmmmmmmmmmmmmmmmmmmmmmmm
mmmmmmmmmmmmmmmmmmmmmmmmmmmm
mmmmmmmmmmmmmmmm

—says we should visit the Amphitheatre the Basin and the Island Tank

—mmmmmmm—OW!

—Oh! I'm sorry I didn't see you there.

This oblivious tourist in chartreuse warmup suit has used her immense girth to knock me out of my zone and has likely damaged my potential career as a frozen mime. Nevertheless, still transcendent, I will avoid venting any anger and take this opportunity to head for the famous next stop in my guide the famous Ponte Vecchio.

Crowds thickening nearer the Arno, Bo imagining himself a sleek powerful Chinook swimming easily through schools of fat herring. Here is the bridge with its shops outboard, most of which seem to specialize in gold jewelry, let's see what I could buy—holy shit! $3000 for a skinny bracelet. For what. Bring up from memory the moment fabricated in countless advertisements. He presents the adornment, her eyes widen with the tacit declaration that *you are the man of my dreams* and *I am now meltingly yours completely and forever or at least until the novelty wears off and then you will buy me something much more expensive.*

The Gardens inundated by a backed-up mass of young field trippers, Bo walking half way around without finding a way to sneak in. Why would I want to pay to look at plants anyway, at home I can row my skiff in to the beach any time I want and get lost in a moss covered rain forest for free. Enough of this, I'm going to take off down this side street, along this poor sluggish dirty river imprisoned between concrete banks, a couple of perched cormorants a hopeful sign that at least some little fish live in its water. And yet here's an unexpected pleasure, a small bar-restaurant with decent prices posted outside…nice and light within…and a convivial atmosphere, the perfect spot to take the edge off the weary tourist's famishment with a bowl of tomato basil soup and perhaps a glass of this Barolo which, it being so good, I'll have a bottle to take along.

CHAPTER 10

The Piazza del Duomo and the Santa Maria del Fiore Cathedral with its famous dome. How lame a tourist I am it is now getting late in the afternoon and I have not paid my way into a single famous must-see example of ancient architectural prowess or aesthetic sensibility or hubris and now I have left as my last opportunity a cathedral. Photos of which I probably was subjected to in the dozens as well as windy descriptions when I was nine.

Stop whining the line is not long just go ahead. But wait what is this small discreet sign by a little door over here which has no line at all it's the climb to the top of the dome up a stairway built inside the walls with its 443 steps this is much more my speed.

The stairs inside built not at all for speed, sometimes uneven, sometimes proceeding up a straight flight and at others in a tight spiral. The odd small clump of other climbers huffing and puffing and happy to pull aside on the narrow landings to let Bo pass. Two sixty-two, two sixty-three…what's this, one emerges into the dome's interior on a narrow platform that leads half way around, giving a great view of this mural that fills the dome—eeeyewww there is some sick stuff going on here, this horned guy smashing a naked person's face with a skull-sized ball, someone nearby being impaled with an eight-foot shaft, beyond that another devil gleefully strangling his victim. I don't really believe I'm destined for hell but this is beginning to depress. If I climb higher it looks like there's another walkway where the scene is more placid. Aha, this must be Jesus himself, with the perfectly white robe and the golden light beaming out from his head, I guess doing the judging. And all these people standing around him with blank or grim expressions. I suppose it would be kind of stressful waiting to see whether you get to stay up here and hang with God, or report below to have your entrails ripped out. Christ! I wonder if there's something wrong with me. I believe I'm supposed to feel exalted up here at this level but it all just seems grim. Maybe I need to get even higher.

Eighty more steps up, Bo emerging into daylight and a view to the south over countless tile-roofed buildings receding to distant hills. The possible presence of a vindictive God much less out here. I suppose Ingrid is traveling in this direction I wonder how far she's gotten—wow that's the first I've thought of her in several hours I must be healing. Maybe I can blame these feelings of spiritual oppression on her disappearance. Although looking at it that way it's not much of a trade. Maybe if I go around to the other side for a view north toward the Ostello San Gallo it'll help me get a restorative sense of place. And a reminder that soon I'll be planning my trip to hike in the Dolomiti. Where, if there were a God, he might approve that I take much more pleasure in his own personal granite creations than in these which some Florentines assumed would curry his favor.

So, around and under this arch I should be able to see…I should see…well, I can see the railway station and hence, somewhere nearby, the Ostello, but distractingly in the foreground is a long haired female person in a short dark skirt alone gazing pensively out over the railing. Whom the idea of approaching is at once compelling and strangely scary.

Perhaps if I retreat briefly back through the arch I can compose myself and produce a plausible excuse for starting a conversation. In which, directness would be the best component, as in, 'could you help me pick out the place I'm staying? That is, if you know the city. Or are you a traveler like myself, looking for inspiration in these ancient bricks and stones. But excuse me, I fear I become disingenuous since in truth I find very little in the way of spiritual uplift, probably due to my much greater affinity for the natural world. Which I suppose may be incomprehensible to someone like yourself who is here out of choice rather than as in my case because it is on the way to somewhere else?' And if I go on in this vein I will have swallowed my foot clear up to the kneecap. Which could be a good thing because it will throttle my attempt to communicate in Spanalian. Which will have tagged me right away as a fool.

But I digress. How about, 'can you help me locate my lodging' that will be enough, and if I survive this start unscorned I can follow by asking advice on a place to get supper. What's the Italian word for supper. Cena in Spanish, come on, you were studying these on the plane…cena, it's the same. But is that a 'ch' or a hard 'c'…with a following i it's ch, like ciao…but what about e…Jesus this is ridiculous just get on out there if this is meant to happen it will happen even if you use Lithuanian…not that I know even one word in Lithuanian… although there must be some words that are common even to English…borscht maybe…okay, okay, I'm going. Although I might take a minute to admire the sculpted footing on this arch—okay.

Around to the north side and—vacancy. No persons, female or male, attractive or repulsive, just a different set of roofs fading toward dull green hills, the implacable featureless sky.

Mood now as grey as the cloud cover, Bo grumbling back to other side of the cupola and the stairway down. Well that was stupid. And now I have to again pass through this depressing Judgment Day scene. Well at least gravity's with me this way. At least as far as this upper landing where God hangs out. What the hell, maybe the bumper stickers on the back decks of the more respectable members of the fleet are right, 'attitude makes the difference'? Why be gloomy? Why not identify with these uptight-looking burghers crowding around as the sacred finger consigns some poor asshole to an eternity of torture? Why get hung up on the fact that the only people in this whole scene who seem to be enjoying themselves are the sadistic devils? And I guess a few hornblowing cherubs. Realistically, neither of which I would hope to join, leaving only—ah fuck it, this is just some centuries-old grim vision anyway, let's proceed on down past the nether region and head back to the hostel, the Dolomites plan, right — what's this? A corporeal sinner? Holy shit, it's her!

Seated on brick step, leaning back, eyes closed holding shoeless ankle, the woman lately of the parapet. Bo nearing in concern.

—Ahh...e enferme? Necesita ayuda?

Eyes opening, appraising

—I have twisted my ankle. And I suppose I could use some help.

How is it that everyone immediately knows English is my

—Can you put any weight on it? You could lean on me. And maybe we'll find someone else on the way down to support your other side?

—I tried, no. And it's just closing, we're likely the only ones left. Maybe the attendant will make a last walk through...or maybe not.

— Well, maybe...I think maybe I could carry you if you want to try.

—That would be better than sitting here all night, wouldn't it. If you don't drop me.

—Okay, let's try. Piggy-back, do you know that word?

—I think I know its meaning.

—Your English is really good.

—I grew up in Chicago.

—Oh, I thought...okay, I'll get below and if you can just lean forward I'll hoist—there. Can you hold this bottle?

Bo under load descending slowly. Not too bad, about like carrying a couple of 60 pound cannonball weights. Sherpas do this all day. Uphill too but I think I'll stick to down. Here's our first level respite with God indicating the way—down. And here's where He tells us to go, amidst the torture.

—What is your name?

—Mariella.

—Hi. I'm Bo. That scene—it's so fiendish!

—Yes, I know. Isn't it wonderful?

Wonderful? Maybe from some other point of view...one I can't really imagine...but speaking of wonder, how about this immediate warm scene. Ten minutes ago she was an unattainable ideal and now her legs are wrapped around my waist. Though this position probably isn't in the Kama Sutra. Getting to be painful, actually, now we're back on the downstairs. Hum some distracting tune...

I'll never be
Your beast of burden
I've walked for miles
My feet are hurtin'

All I want is
For you to make love to me…

—What's that?

—Oh, oops, just a song.

— How are you holding up, it is very nice of you to do this.

—Okay…look this is the last flight. And there's your attendant.

—Visitors must leave the Duomo before 5 o'clock. But perhaps you are blind and unable to read either Italian or English, which as you can see the notice is printed in both?

Barrage of Italian from just behind Bo's ear, the rebuker wilting and jumping to hold open the door. Passing out into the dusky piazza, Bo carefully lowering his cargo to lean against wall, flexing fatigue out of back and legs.

—So now what?

—My car is not too far that way, if you think you can manage.

—Sure, let's go.

Past staring remnant tourists, out of the Piazza and along the Via Proconsulo, turning onto Via Corso…proceeding to Via Pandolfini… several more plodding blocks and stopping again.

—Not too far, you said?

—I did not want to discourage you. It's impossible to park in the town center. We're almost there, just up that next street to the right.

Nearly exhausted, Bo steeling himself to finish

this last leg with some spirit. Stopping at last before a green Jensen Healy which he drives to a courtyard off Avda. Vittorio Alfieri. Helping up broad stairs to a second floor apartment, profuse thanks, brief exchange of names and histories and an offer to safekeep the Barolo if he would like to return for supper tomorrow. Bo close to floating along the empty streets on his way home. The way she looked at me when she suggested dinner, fingers gently tugging my shirt, I think something very nice could happen here.

CHAPTER 11

Next night, the Barolo going very well with a complex herb-seasoned seafood pasta and a backdrop of intricate Bach piano harmonies. An ostello you must be hardy to endure the young and callous backpacking crowd. Well yes but they are not all like that. The wine's effect paralleling a growing sense of possibility manifested after meal's finish by a collaborative almost dancelike washing of dishes. Eyes on eyes at the door, Mariella's deep and brown, Bo assaying a gentle first kiss. Sense that more could occur this night, but better to let it happen slowly and naturally. You intend to be back from your mountains Thursday evening, I hope you will call, then oh yes I will.

This new name singing in Bo's heart on walk through empty streets back to bunk. A song continuing unabated over the long drive north the next day through Ferrara and Padova and the steepening ascent up a winding forested two lane road. Bo joining other adventurous drivers challenging the curves. As one might accelerate into helpless infatuation…

…Mariella…

Nearing the Austrian border, a room at a small family inn, dinner conversation all in German. Late next morning parking car and hiking up through lush meadows, past belled sheep and cows. Their tinkling and clanking still faintly audible from far above as the steepening trail finds a way up into the granite massif. Then leveling on a broad shelf to pass through boulder fields, majestic peaks rising skyward. Bo occasionally detouring to scramble up a minor crag. Perched vertiginous thrill of being surrounded above and below by air and space…

…Mariella…

A yearning that only increases through the week. Healthy good spirits of other hikers at dinner in the refugios somehow foolish. How can they use so many words in superficial conversation when there is only one spoken sound that has any real meaning. Her name a sigh through the grasses at lower elevations, throaty in the small slides Bo's boots set off on steeper slopes…Mariella…even in the thunderbolt of the intense sudden rainstorm that overtakes him as he hauls himself up a steep cabled col above Refugio Fanes. And in the pounding of his heart as he hurries back down through crack of thunder and lightning shattered cloud, desperate to reach the inn and safety so as not to die before finding out what comes next…

…Mariella…

Driving back down through Cortina and Castello

and the steep winding stretch above Canazei. Groups of adrenaline seeking couples on ninja motorcycles passing with insane risk even on the corners, their infectious recklessness slinging Bo into a few insecure passes of his own in hopes of making Firenze by evening.

Their first night together surpassing even his separation-fevered imaginings. A long embrace in the kitchen leading to abandonment of dinner preparation and in her bed Bo entering reverently and reaching an awed sense of physical fit so perfect that they might have been designed for one another. Her abandon unlike anything he'd known before, manifested in a moaning that Bo could not quite tell if it was aloud or vibrating within his inner senses.

Most of the following several days spent in sensual exploration. Bo swept along in her willingness to commit all toward finding the maximum of pleasure, mind blown in the variety of position and assumed personalities played so fully as to become reality. One time, spiraling into a fierce frenzy with Bo emerging scratched and bitten but more often languorous, carefully telling the story until just before the conclusion, slowing and lying in close embrace, moving just enough to prolong the state of exquisite anticipation.

Eventually a sense of surfacing, a discovery that day to day life had continued on. Bo's residence in the apartment taken as a fait accompli. Mariella going off mornings to teach her music history classes at the American University, returning late afternoons to Bo and their investigations of the body-mind interface. Their communion reaching so deep that sometimes when they were touching Bo could not tell where his skin left off and hers began.

Bo beginning to think more elaborately about meals than what café to briefly visit before returning to bed. Leaving Mariella's neighborhood through increasingly wide concentric wanderings, getting to know the grocery and wine shops and taking the role of quartermaster and supper chef. Days happily becoming weeks. Discussions trending forward, possibility raised of Mariella joining Bo in Alaska for next summer's salmon season, an idea that grows in his mind until the future becomes as full of happiness as the present.

Until a Tuesday afternoon when a slight discordant note attends Mariella's arrival home. A subtle air of distraction growing over the course of the following week into a noticeable reserve, a degree of separation from the union Bo has come to believe permanent. His concern, finally voiced, getting an unsatisfying explanation of challenges at work, leaving the sense there must be more.

Bo, left alone in his total commitment, turning over possibilities and theorizing a possible stultifying effect of his near constant presence, his failure to bring anything new into the relationship. That finding work of some sort might address. Pursuing through his limited contacts with little progress until Mariella's suggestion that a professor colleague at the University had need of help on a project.

Bo showing up early on campus to mingle with foreign exchange students filling the walkways between classes. Finally finding the astronomy department incongruously located in the basement of a 15th century villa. Giovanni, Mariella's colleague, a handsome impeccably dressed Italian-American from New York. Showing Bo around and explaining the job which turns out to be peering into a computer screen. Comparing blown-up thermal images of sections of the universe relayed from orbiting telescopes, the goal to find any anomalies that might indicate the presence of an unseeable orbiting planet. Bo to be one of many thousands so engaged. A job that could be left to search programs—and which, indeed, was being so performed—but which it was suspected might benefit from the more random perceptions of the human eye.

Tedious work but bearable, considering it could be Bo who finds the grail of a planet hospitable to life. Potential for fame insufficient, however, to counter his unease when his absence each day fails to restore Mariella's full intimacy. Concluding after several more weeks of the same low-level discord that a longer break was needed. Announcing intent to cycle, on the Aprilia he'd bought to replace the rented Fiat, to Cinque Terre over the weekend. Mariella endorsing the idea, warmly kissing Bo goodbye after a lazy Saturday morning breakfast.

Bo setting off on the three-hour ride, happy with the mild day and the prospect of renewal. Getting as far as the outskirts of La Spezia before the engine begins to cut out. Alarmed, leaving the highway before the bike comes to an unrevivable stop. Bo pushing it around town, at last finding a mechanic who, yes, could fix it, but would need a part which would not come before Monday.

Bo finding a café for lunch near the commercial docks and practicing his crow-eating delivery before calling to ask Mariella for a ride back. No answer then, nor halfway back at one of the innumerable stops on the slow bus route to Firenze. Nor at eight o'clock, from the downtown terminus. Climbing out of a taxi and entering the courtyard from the avenue just as a BMW Bo recognizes as his employer's arrives through the motor entrance. Bo watching appalled as Giovanni opens the passenger door. Helps Mariella out and escorts her, arm around waist, up the steps to the front door. Ensuing disagreement, Giovanni clearly wanting to go in and Mariella resisting, finally guiding him back to car and a long kiss before disappearing inside.

Violent impulses race through Bo's mind and subside, leaving him empty and shaken. Sinking onto stone bench and considering. This looks bad, looks worse than bad, but perhaps there is some innocent explanation? Best to confront head on. Gather self control, go and find out.

Inside, working past denial and harsh words through tears to a confession: Mariella's deep entanglement over the past year. Giovanni's avowed intent to leave his incompatible wife, who'd remained in Ravenna after he'd taken the job in Firenze. Then, his two-month leave taken to go back and "work things out". Mariella's avowal to end the affair, made just weeks before meeting Bo and the beginning of their blissful time together. A time that she was sure had superseded her ties to Giovanni, until his recent return with solemn declaration of a new devotion only to her. Which knocked her off balance once again.

And yes, they had slept together earlier that day. But she would not let him in to the apartment where she and Bo had shared such intimacy. And now she did not know what to do. Did not know how she felt. Did not know what was to come.

Bo having even less in the way of answers. Knowing nothing but these new depths of sorrow, and a continuing attachment so strong that compassion at her distress overrules self interest. Passing again through anger and sinking into the couch to stare at the floor. Mariella after some moments sitting close and stroking his hair, his neck, arms, leading him to bedroom and drawing him in to a state of helpless devotion in which he gives himself to her as absolutely in this new atmosphere of pain as he had before in happiness.

Waking to sun through window oblivious for a moment until the fact of her betrayal strikes as an almost physical blow. Fighting it off and looking for some solution. How about if we go to Cinque Terre together, get away and decide what's to come. Why not. Yes that's a good idea. I will arrange to be away and we can leave this morning.

Circling around the issue on the drive west and then, in a blue walled room on one of Manarola's narrow streets, Bo steadily losing ground through alternating arguments and lovemaking. Their walks along the paths through hillside gardens and olive groves and atop the cliffs between Corniglia and Riomaggiore, the Mediterranean heaving and frothing far below offering some respite but not enough, nowhere near enough, until on the way back to Firenze his announced intent to return to Alaska eliciting her tears but no attempt to dissuade.

A miserable night spent on the sofa, packed bag at his feet. At the station in the morning one last embrace, her body yielding, her mind refusing to admit any way out of their torn state.

The long train ride back to Rome, sky lowering to match Bo's dispirited gloom. An endless flight west, the British Airways jet fruitlessly chasing the sun. Bo downing a procession of 7 & 7s, losing count somewhere over Alberta. Drinking steadily through the afternoon at SeaTac waiting for the evening flight north and its own collection of little bottles. Very nearly falling into the harbor while climbing on to the Walter at Thompson Harbor and then waking up to the stench of his own puke. A subsequent vow to never again sleep aboard when drunk. Adherence to which proving a rare accomplishment, through subsequent long dark winter months, spent as often as not seriously inebriated in Lincoln and Quixote, attempt to forget producing only futility.

PART THREE

Sitka

CHAPTER 12

Loud pounding above jerking Bo back into the present, sound of the wheelhouse door sliding open and then Gary's voice

—Hey Bo we're gonna be taking off in 45 or so, you still want—

Face appearing in hatch opening above engine room steps.

—to come with…you napping down here?

—Ahh. Just…contemplating my next move.

—I see…well? So?

—So…holler again on your way out? I want to finish changing the filters.

—Not a problem.

Bo filling a new filter with diesel and spinning it onto the engine. Thanks Gary for the well timed interruption, might've spent all afternoon miserating about...okay, leave it. Forty-five minutes, should have time to warm up the engine and at least get the old oil pumped out. Assuming I haven't introduced an air lock in which case I'll have to spend the rest of the night with the manual trying to figure out how to bleed this sucker. I mean, pardon me, this exceptionally well made and reliable engine which has gotten me into many productive circumstances and which will now as I press this button start right up? Oh good.

Bo removing to the wheelhouse to avoid the Cummins rumble until the temp gauge passes 170. Should be unviscous enough now, shut down and position this empty five gallon bucket and open the hose valve and start this familiar tedious work. Counting strokes of the hand pump toward the 110 which it takes on average. Sixty is where my right arm begins to ache, change to my left which is nowhere near as coordinated and gets tired quickly and so I switch back and endure the pain. A nice little 12-volt Jabsco pump would help, I could mount it right here on this bulkhead but wait there's that slurping noise, air entering the hose at last I'm done. Hundred and twenty-three, what's so prime about that number—

—Blam blam blam hey Bo I'm heading up, go pick up Julie and some others, you ready?

—Well…how would it be if I meet you at the turnoff? I gotta clean up and stop at the Lakeside, what can I bring?

—Aw, we've got plenty of fish and brats…you could bring some beer.

—Got it. I'll see you in a few.

* * *

Bo arriving first at the rendezvous, hucking a case

of IPA off the seat as Gary's king cab swerves in. Bill Sheridan and wife Elizabeth up front along with Gary's wife Julie. Greetings.

—We're pretty full up here, you mind riding in back with the others?

—Sure don't.

Circling to pull open the camper door and climb in. Couple of young guys stretched out on the bunk forward, Gary's deckhands. And perched on a bench behind, its—

—Myra?

—Bo! How cool! Gary said he was bringing one of his fishing friends but I had no idea it would be you!

—Yeah, me neither…hi Nick, Charlie. Well I guess there's still room in here for me and my beer.

Taking the bench opposite Myra who launches into conversation.

—I was covering the last Borough Council meeting, this was before Bill switched me from the canine beat saying I was too emotionally involved, and Gary was there and we got to talking afterwards and he invited me to come today. Don't you just love his twin Corgis and isn't it a freaky coincidence his wife is best friends with Bill's wife—

Gesturing animatedly in blue jeans, soft white shirt under partially buttoned blue cardigan. How is it, she begins to talk and I stop hearing. Something to do with the dog preoccupation, maybe. Not that I am totally inattentive for example I note that although certainly no movie star she is actually not bad looking and not just because of her chest which though modestly covered today is undeniably—wait is it fishing she's on to?

—so I need to find out and you're probably the perfect person, what's a sea pooey?

—Sea pooey? I, uh, I never heard of a sea pooey.

—Me either but that's what Laurie at Fish and Game told me was the biggest factor in their decision, that there was a really big sea pooey in one of their catch areas last week. Salisbury Sound! That's where it was.

—Ha ha, Fish and Game found a really big sea pooey in Salisbury Sound that's—wait a minute, what decision?

—You know, what I was talking about, to open up the inside fishery one more time next Tuesday.

—Shit all Friday. This is really happening. She say anything about Rick Corvis?

—I'm not sure, I'd have to look at my notes. She did say the department is trying to take fishermen's input more seriously.

—Yeah, right. Jesus. Well look, sea pooey, it's not…it has to be one of those acronymic words the bureaucrats like to invent, like fannie mae. CPUE is catch per unit of effort, they take how many boats fished, for how many days, and divide it into how many fish they caught. Supposed to be an indication of abundance—holy shit they based it entirely on my last trip didn't they, that is so stupid—let's stop talking about this I'm gonna get a brain cramp. And anyway we're here.

All tumbling out of the truck to help start salmon and sausages on a slow grill before cracking beers and beginning a game of sub-ultimate Frisbee across the bowl shaped meadow. The play proceeding amiably, Myra finding an inordinate number of opportunities to bump into Bo. A not unpleasant sensation accompanied by green eyes flashing mischievously. Scoring relatively even until someone follows an out of bounds throw into the parking lot.

—Uh oh. Sign says this is a rare example of fragile sub-alpine meadow please stay on the trails.

—Uh oh.

—Uh oh.

—Oh well. Food's probably ready anyhow.

—Time for another beer too.

The group regathering, loading paper plates.

—This is a really nice fish, Gary. You can afford to eat your own large kings?

—Aw, a damn sea lion gnawed on it just as I was pulling it up to the boat. Plant might've given me a decent number two price, but a person's got to eat.

—Well, we won on that deal.

Bill interjecting.

—Actually we won. Big time. It was about eight to three, I think.

—What do you mean, despite repeated illegal blocks (ahem!) I scored at least three myself. Probably four. I remember them all, each one a magnificent leaping feat of athleticism. You're going to report on this for the next edition, right?

—Well Bo your scoring in the B.S. competition is

certainly newsworthy.

—Bo, you want to climb that little peak when we're done?

—Sure, Myra...you really want to?

The trail up steepening before disappearing into the rock, the route the rest of the way clear and well-worn with just enough tricky spots to heighten the senses. Finding a perch just below the jagged top to marvel at Sitka Sound below, evening sun glimmering off the breeze-swirled surface, the rounded cone of Mount Edgecumbe in the right hand distance.

—You're pretty agile for a journalist...for a, for a, grrr

—Go ahead, you can say girl, I don't mind. Men are so cute when they're condescending.

—I usually say 'person of the female persuasion' to avoid offense. Are you a climber?

—Not really. It just feels, normal. My dad worked for the forest service and we lived on a little ranch out of town in the Bannock Range. I guess you could say my parents were into gender equality from early on—my older brothers were super hyper, and when they were kicked out of the house, which was all the time, I got kicked out with them. I didn't really have any choice but to keep up.

—Well it could come in handy in case the Watchdog assigns you to the central Baranof beat. Course, you'd be covering the deer and bear communities, not many people up there. Actually, not any. I bet you could climb that direction up and over and all the way down to Chatham Strait and not see anyone.

Contemplating the range of peaks to the east, patches of snow pink-tinged in the late evening sunlight.

—I think I'll stick to Sitka at least for a while longer. Looks pretty cold up there. It's getting cold here too, let's go down now?

Back in the parking lot, most of the cooking gear stowed away, the others finishing their beers. Across the lot a green Mustang reverberating a woofered bass beat, bit of sweet smoke escaping tinted windows.

—Nice timing you two. You'll have the back to yourselves, some of Nick and Charlie's friends showed up, they're going to hang with them.

—You don't worry they'll, ahh, go astray?

They know the drill, fishing comes first and the boat's off limits for drinking or whatever. Long as they're ready to work when I need them, I'm not gonna tell them how to play, pretend I know alcohol's good and pot's bad. I think they're just trying on the thug posture, see what it feels like. Ready to roll?

Snaking down the steep switchbacked road, narrow darkening passage through second growth forest looming on either side. Myra perched cross legged on the bunk, facing Bo on the bench, combating the gloom with animated exposition.

—Oh I have to tell you how the Borough meeting went. It was fantastic! The Commissioners were really sympathetic, at least until that Hans Kuchen went on and on about people's right to an undisturbed night's sleep, and I think they were wavering but one of the members of the Associated Sitka K9 Pooch Club had volunteered to bring two vanloads of folks from the Pioneer Rest Home for an outing, and they all stood up one by one and told their sweet stories about the pets they used to have and how much they missed them. And when the Commission called an advisory vote it was overwhelming. So they're developing a supportive resolution. Isn't that great?

—Uh look Myra. I should tell you, I don't really like dogs.

Her expression incredulous...passing into relief.

—Oh I'm sure that's not true or at least you just haven't met the right kind of dog.

Palms up in gesture of appeal, Bo preparing to elaborate on the species' negatives—cloying obsequiousness, paranoia toward strangers, mindless barking, insistence on depositing feces in public spaces. The truck slamming over an unseen bump, Myra abruptly pitching forward arms out catching herself against Bo's shoulders her breasts briefly settling into his uplifted hands.

Recovering, gazes meeting, embarrassment overshadowed by something more. Your smile even in this dim light is so sweet my heart grins in response. If I slide closer and take your hand will it be all right? if we explore each other's fingertips will it smooth the lurching ride, will I lose myself in the moment and forget yes I think yes.

Transport ending as Gary swerves in next to Bo's truck. Myra assuming a businesslike attitude.

— I need to get home and finish up this fishing story, we're trying to get it into tomorrow's edition. I'll probably be working on it till really late. You think I should call that Rick you were talking about? What's his last name?

— C O R V I S, he's in the book. Yeah, you should talk to him. He'll give you an earful...would you...like a ride home?

—Sure that'd be great. I'm just up on the south end of Seward Street.

At the Katlian light, Bo honking at Gary and turning to cruise the waterfront. The dark gear store, glare of lights from the fish plant, farther along in front of the P bar a handful of smokers on the sidewalk eerie in a pool of blue light from beer signs. Bo driving slowly around the church and up the hill, exploring a developing suspicion that the friendly creature sharing his pickup cab might be deeper than first impression.

—So...you're off the dog beat, you said?

—Oh—yeah. Maybe I did get a little carried away, this being my first try at news writing. I thought I had to make sure Mrs. Brafly—she was my first contact—was happy with the story. Which, as Bill explained, isn't really the point. And I do like dogs, a lot. When I was little, growing up way out of town, my best friend was a black lab. Now tell me, Bo, is it true? You don't like them at all?

—Well uh...

Bo dissembling, surprised at a new moderate voice trying to hijack his tongue.

...I suppose I can understand that some people might value the idea of unquestioning love. But I can't use it. I don't look for friends that only tell me what I want to hear, and I don't have any need to be slobbered on when I've had a bad day. Maybe there's some smart, considerate, unobtrusive breed out there but I haven't seen it. And these fatuous little things people carry around like designer handbags. Or walk around thinking it's cute when they yap and snarl at whoever comes near, Jesus Christ it makes you—

Sensing a rant approaching, trying to back off.

—So. Anyway. Only one semi-tolerable dog I've known, a German Shepherd mix that a girlfriend I had a few years ago owned, and even it—in the off season, when Shelly went to work I spent a fair amount of time with it, and of course it barked way too much...but it loved chasing sticks, and I didn't mind tossing them. But it obstinately refused to bring them back. Just part way, and then it'd leer at me, I guess thinking I'd wrestle for it or something. Which there's no way, so I'd just go back inside and leave the dog out in the cold, alone. Never learned. That's a dog, isn't it? Focused entirely on short-term profit—oh, here's the end of Seward. I guess this is your place, huh?

Pulling over next to a gray two-story building. Myra leaning back against her door, regarding him with a broad disconcerting smile.

—Gee, Bo. You can be kind of obtuse on this

topic, can't you. A German Shepherd is no kind of a retriever. You're lucky he would play with you at all!

—Oh yeah, right—

—But I get your point about some of the little dogs. Especially the overbred ones. I'm definitely not into Westminster.

—What's that? Westminster? Where the queen lives?

—No, goofy, it's where the big purebred show happens every year. You know, where you and your hired expert would take your Basenji, which you had been grooming and training and beautifying for months, to parade before the judges…but…maybe I'm disturbing you?

—You do seem to have an exceptionally depraved imagination.

—All in fun, Bo. I've got to go in now and get to work. That was great today. Maybe we'll get together again?

—Sure…life is pretty hectic right now, with a short opener and then the July first season, but we'll see how it goes?

—Sounds good. Bye, Bo.

Bo checking the time after Myra's door closes. Forty-five minutes until Reilly's flight lands. Drive back and check out the Lakeside, should maybe get some more beer since I left the remnants of that case with Gary. A few cars in the lot, lights still on, looks open. Funny how other-worldly a grocery store seems late at night, garish abundance of food in the stark light just sitting here disregarded. Brightcolored tomatoes and limes crying out to be noticed. So sad. As long as I'm on patrol I might as well buy a few things to get Reilly started in the morning, eggs bread jam.

Lights in the airport bright and glaring as well after the dark drive over the bridge and across Japonski Island. The flight from Juneau delayed, Bo happy enough to pass time at the café counter with a piece of raspberry pie. And muse over this obtrusive Myra whose green eyes linger. And what first seemed like persistent nattering maybe a sheen over a more elemental cleverness? And who possesses another attractive feature or two which it would be nice to explore. Should I wish to complicate my simple fucked up life, coping with the desertion of someone I'm incapable of forgetting.

Will the owner of a pair of deep brown eyes please report to emotional baggage claim. Items not retrieved after 180 days will be obsessed.

There's the announcement that Reilly's plane is landing. Good to see her brassy self again. At least no worries of complications there, Lucky to have a deckhand who is not only diligent hardworking and congenial but easy on the eyes as well. And stably coupled up with her fellow graduate student in Arizona. Which led to some discomfort last year, being in close quarters with a woman who is off limits but I'm over it.

Bo heading for the deplaning area, joining a handful of fishing and hunting guides, here to pick up their clients who now file through the access door and bunch up. A scrum of paunchy guys in camo here to forget the law firm, the parts counter, the insurance office, by hooking and slicing and blasting the crap out of whatever scale- or fur-covered animal presents itself. Not that my life is mayhem free but—

—Bo!

—Hey, Reilly!

And here she is, blond hair tailing out under watch cap, creating even in cargo pants and dark wool shirt her own zone of rawboned attractiveness amongst the crowd. A giant hug, recapitulation of events since last season's close as the baggage belt rumbles into movement and transports nothing at all for a good five minutes before parading a jumble of suitcases duffels backpacks and gun cases.

—There's one! One out of two, not bad for Alaska…and there's the other yippee.

Bo hoisting one oversized duffel bag and a carry-on day pack, Reilly with laptop case and the other bag, finding the truck backed into a space ready to roll. Reilly remarking as the road soars over the Harbor bridge toward town

—Can't see too well but it doesn't look like Sitka's changed much.

—Not downtown. Some development out by the Post Office. Handful of new longliner mini-McMansions scattered around. Basically though she's the same old town. You want to stop and get a beer? Or I've got some for the boat.

—I don't know, I had to get up at four to start the cheap flight I patched together from Flagstaff. What

I'd really like to do, hit the rack and be ready for tomorrow. What's on the agenda?

—Well, have to finish the oil change, shouldn't take too long. There's always gear to tie up. I'd like to sand and paint the cockpit coaming, maybe some fresh varnish on the wheelhouse windows…damn. I wonder what's the chance of getting enough dry weather to do that before this stupid hatchery opening I guess is going to happen next Tuesday.

—Stupid? What's stupid about getting to fish? I heard you did real good on the last one.

—Jesus, even in Arizona you heard? Who told you?

—Neva, you know the deckhand on the Carrie, we message.

—Yeah well. The fleet thinks I've got the touch but I just lucked into a place with a lot of fish and no boats, I don't think that'll happen again this time. Anyway, here we are. Grab a cart, we'll get your gear down to the boat. There's some breakfast stuff here, I'll probably show up around eight, we can get started.

Bo driving back along Katlian after settling Reilly in the focsle. A plague of problematic women. Reilly, engaged...and kind of a know-it-all at times with her studies, never know when she'll start going off about Hume or some such…Myra, mercurial, though it now seems this dispiriting dog fixation doesn't go as deep as I'd thought…worst of all Mariella who is five thousand miles away and not acknowledging my existence. And then there's Karen…shit, maybe better to have no prospects at all, free to fantasize instead of starving in the midst of plenty. Not all that late, wonder what Wade's up to. Could go look in at the Quixote. But don't really feel like getting drunk…too confused to get wasted, that's funny. Confused and needy. Maybe I'll just inhabit this state of mind for a change. Just go home.

Plane of light in the hallway from Karen's room door ajar. Homer pushing through to rub against legs, Bo stooping to return the friendly gesture, scratch behind ears. Thanks for not barking.

—Hi Karen.

—Hi there Bo. How are you doing.

—Okay. Or, not. I don't know. Pretty angst-ridden.

—Maybe you need a nice cup of hot chocolate and a cookie.

—I don't think so. I should maybe just dive into it. Go read some Sartre or….

—Bo.

—Yeah.

—You could come in here.

—Yeah.

Karen turning down the light, Bo shucking clothes to climb into soft sheets and welcoming arms. Finding a sweet corner between neck and pillow, press face into this dark warm space fragrant with skin and shampoo, let me just sink into oblivion and let the hunger move from mind downward, hand roaming this ample body. Karen an easy lover…Bo following an imperative for speed…a preliminary qualifying run…spinning the tires to lay down traction…then riding the clutch out smooth and flooring the throttle fishtailing at first then steadying faster and then faster and faster hitting three hundred at the quarter…the chute popping out…coasting slowly to a stop…my God that was…

My God I am lost.

Bo rolling to one side. Later after Karen's breathing has subsided to regularity, after long minutes staring into the darkness, slipping carefully from under the covers and down the hall to climb into his own bed and endure alternating visions of eyes first brown, then green…these eyes have me… why can't I be satisfied with a generous woman like Karen who consistently treats me well…but on some basic level something lacking. Always looking for the ideal, the chances of attaining are what.

I could get lucky. Or I could wind up searching till I'm seventy.

CHAPTER 13

Bo gratified on stepping onto the Walter's deck next morning to find the front windows sanded and ready to varnish. And back here, the trolling hatch prepped as well. Following the aroma of fresh coffee into the wheelhouse.

—Reilly, nice work. What an excellent crew you are.

—Aw thanks. The weather looked good so I figured I'd get on it. You have brushes? I found the paint in the back deck locker, but no brushes.

—Let's see...yeah, here they are in this tool drawer with the caulk and stuff. Start with the windows, okay, maybe we can get two coats on today. That coffee smells good—damn, I forgot to get milk, didn't I.

—I got some earlier, it's in the cooler back there. You want eggs? I already ate, but I could fry some more up easy enough.

—No, thanks, I stopped at the Lincoln—wait a minute, this what you're calling milk? Vanilla soy?

—Sure, it's good. Plus, you don't want to go on clogging yourself up with dairy.

—I don't? What'll I clog myself up with then? I don't know about this Reilly, last year it was vegetarian every fourth meal, pretty soon we won't have anything on board but nuts and leaves?

—Now now, there's no need to exaggerate. Just try it!

— I guess it can't be any worse than the powdered stuff. Okay let's see. Bleck. Wait a minute. Hmm. Kinda sweet. Maybe it isn't all that bad.

—See?

—Okay. Maybe I can go with it. But don't tell anybody, all right?

After adding lube oil, Bo prowling the boat with grease gun in hand checking off a mental list of zerk fittings. Should end for end the anchor cable, too, get the uncorroded part out to take the strain. Fire up the Cummins and turn on the hydraulics to lower the 100-pound Furfjord and all this chain and nylon onto the dock so I can stretch out the wire. Wow that makes a big heap to get past.

Trying to be considerate, Bo hovering solicitously at the approach of passersby. Can you make it there. Let me help you get your load past. Sorry about this, should be done in a little while.

Bob on the Icelander, moored nearby, voicing some irritation on his third trip down the dock.

—Doggone it Bo. It's easier to get past your pile of crap here than your cloud of apologies. I'm not an invalid.

—Oh, sure. Sorry for apologizing so much.

—Ha ha. Say, you think Salisbury'll be a good place to start next week?

The work gathering momentum. After getting the anchor line respooled, Bo redescending to engine room to check battery levels and tighten propeller shaft stuffing box. Then back up into June sunshine to touch up the name on the starboard side bow, where a scuffing fender had turned the W into an italic. "*N*alter K", not. Whine of disc and orbital sanders and circular saws from boats nearby, exhaust mutter of freezer boats' auxiliaries, shouts and occasional laughter of crews working earnestly in anticipation of the July king season.

Later, Reilly glossing the last section of the aft hatch, Bo stepping out onto the dock to admire. White hull paint applied during last month's haulout gleaming in afternoon sunlight, set off by dark green trim of guards, rails, name and hatch coamings.

A resonant voice heralding Arguello's arrival.

—A sight to be proud of, this boat of yours with her sweet classical sheer line. We may be contemplating the highest construct produced by human endeavor. Truly a work of art, yet at the same time a lethal machine designed to wrest from often hostile elements one of the most satisfying foods on the planet. What else can compare? A fighter jet has its own dangerous beauty, but it cannot nurture, only destroys. Yachts, sports cars, svelte but basically frivolous. There is only one thing in the universe that can outclass a troller. Will you hazard a guess?

—A turkey-cranberry sandwich? We worked through lunch, I might be biased…I give up, what.

—I offer a hint: same combination of beauty, danger, and nurturing, only it's been perfected by millennia of evolutionary fine-tuning. Here before us is a lovely example, cleaning out that paintbrush on your fish hatch.

—Hi there Wade. Funny how someone with not a bit of Irish extraction can be so full of blarney.

—Spoken like a disloyal daughter of Erin. But, as always, it is wonderful to gaze on your visage. Bo speaking of sandwiches shall we dine at the Quixote tonight? You owe me, if you recall, a dinner due to the goddamn stupid fucked up opening we're having next Tuesday.

—Somehow that slipped my mind…okay, if we can do it kinda late. Still have plenty of work here, plus I have to hit the gear store.

—Late is fine, more time to build up an appetite for Herman's wife's black cod.

—Damn, forgot about that too. Anyway. Meet out there around 8:30?

—That's fine.

Reilly sanding trim ahead of second varnish coat as Bo inventories fishing gear, then both cooperating on grocery list.

—We'll load up on staples now, enough for a few trips, get the perishable stuff just after we load ice for Tuesday. You ready? I'll drop you off to buy the groceries, then I'll go down to Murray Pacific, pick you up afterwards.

Reilly deposited at the Lakeside with shirt pocket full of cash, Bo pulling onto the wooden wharf to park by the gear store. Aisles crowded. Bo diverted from sizing up lead cannonballs by animated discussion, two trollers in the tackle section arguing optimal hootchie colors.

—These here, twelves, are the best for cohos. No question.

—They don't glow. You've gotta have the glow. Know how dark it is down there? One forty-twos, those work.

Other trollers within earshot, Bo included, suddenly taking deep interest in nearby displays, surreptitiously listening to this daringly open discussion of gear secrets.

—You're crazy. You never took one of them into a closet? They only give off light for at most a minute after they're in the dark. By the time you've got your line down, you're dragging around a plain old dull piece of plastic.

—Whattya mean plain old, it's still got the green, which is all yours have. Plus, the glow can't just shut off sudden, it's has to taper off gradual so you're still getting something.

—The glow, phooey. Better to have something realistic, like an eighty-four, got the dark back, like a herring, fades to lighter blue on the sides—and, it's got the white belly.

—That is effed up. You think a salmon's not gonna be suspicious of something shaped like a squid but colored like a herring?

—All I know is, they work. That's the real measure, isn't it? We buy these things because they look like something we already caught fish with, not because we know what a salmon really sees down there. We can't even be certain about our own perceptions, let alone the fishes'. Like, how do you know it's me talking to you, and not somebody in a dream you're having?

—What? Hell, if this was a dream, I'd have somebody else in it. Someone better looking…smarter, maybe…someone who hadn't been wearing the same smelly shirt since December. But this ain't a dream. You've been reading too much a that philosophy.

—What's too much? It wouldn't hurt you to raise your literary sights a click or two above Big Tits Monthly. Think about it. Like Berkely said, matter might be an illusion—it's only when we sense something about it that it becomes real. Maybe it doesn't even exist, without us.

Eavesdroppers drifting away. Bo looking down at his list. Better get back to reality, that was getting weird. I'm just glad they didn't seem to know about my personal favorites, those sweet seventy-eights, glow-in-the-darks with the green swatches…there's Beethoven on the phone, wonder who this is.

—Bo? Is that you?

—Yeah, but sorry, I don't recognize—

—Bo it's Myra I'm just calling to say I'm sorry we didn't—

—Hang on a minute Myra let me get

outside…there, I was in the gear store, loud in there.

— Bo I didn't mean to leave so abruptly last night, I just get preoccupied when I've got a story to put together…but…I haven't stopped thinking about you how about if we do something together—

A couple of exiting shoppers driving Bo around the corner to lean on truck hood.

—just the two of us maybe dinner? You want to? Maybe tonight?

—Well—sure Myra. Let's. But I can't tonight. How about, tomorrow?

—Oh, that would be great. You want me to meet you? I'm thinking about getting a car, but I don't have one yet, but if I have enough time I can make my own way somewhere.

—I'll pick you up. Around seven sound good?.

—Sure. I'm upstairs, apartment 2B?

—See you there.

Bo reentering store, mind up the hill. Where was I. Cannonballs. Two fifty-pounders, one sixty, two forty-fives. Save all that weight for last, fill this little cart. Box of hot spot flashers. A dozen bronze king spoons. Ball bearing swivels, line snaps, nicopress crimps, lead swivels, stainless hooks, 70-pound and 110-pound leader. And beads and barrel swivels and of course hootchies, with green eyes. No. It's Myra with the green eyes. Her call a more intriguing distraction than that discussion, though they make a nice segue, fishing lures to sex, not necessarily disparate topics either remember that stripper they brought in from Juneau for Gary's bachelor party a couple years ago had hootchies on her nipples which she could swing around in circles …was actually kinda weird. But maybe it would be sexier on someone more available than a stripper. How can it be sexy if you know there's a guaranteed interruptus before you even get to the coitus. Much better paying attention to women with whom there's a real chance. Not that there's a guaranteed chance now with Myra but it looks like it could go that way, I am starting to feel a little loopy when I think of her and it seems like she—

—Excuse me I need to get at these hootchies

Lean wizened Boyd off the Spirit reaching in and grabbing six packs of seventy-eights, fixing Bo with a glittering, ancient eye.

—That was a buncha crap, huh. Ideas define matter? Fah! It's the other way around. You ever read "Leviathan"? Hobbes? It's material objects that cause thoughts. When they intrude on our senses, see, they activate our minds. That guy should've brought that up, woulda shut up his smartass friend quick.

Receding down the aisle with perilously shambling gait.

Wow, that was…damn, my secret hootchie has been outed. Where was I, oh yeah heading for the trolling wire. Where's the two-fathom marked. Should replace it all, six hundred-fathom spools. Holy shit the price went up again—don't think about it. Okay, along here and hoist the leads onto the bottom of the cart and go donate a large chunk of my big king trip in exchange for this tiny volume of gear how come this stuff is so expensive.

Bo returned to the tangible while paying and loading gear into truck, but thoughts straying again on way to grocery. If Myra's a real possibility...maybe polygamy works for some but I can't figure out how to keep it from getting crazy with two, let alone three, Mariella pulling me from the past, now Myra in the future and Karen in some weird in between. Something's got to give...this thing with Karen that pretends to not be a thing. I should extricate. Maybe I can work it out with her with no hard feelings. When. Why not now.

Bo pulling up to store entrance, Reilly with two full shopping carts.

—Hope you didn't have to wait long.

—Not too long. Here's your change.

—Three dollars is all? Jesus it's not just gear gone through the roof, it's food too.

—I got a big pack of gum, it wasn't on the list.

—That must explain it. Look, I've got to take off for a while. Let's cart this stuff down to the boat, then can I leave you to get it stowed away? I'll come back and we can go out to the Quixote for dinner?

—Sure I can do that.

* * *

Bo grabbing the bicycle. Maybe riding will get me pumped up for this onerous visit. Maybe a couple of Obsidian Stouts will calm me down once I get there, make a quick stop back at the Lakeside. Forgot the backpack. But I can put them down inside my shirt. Brr cold. This little hill up Lake street will get my blood flowing, maybe upwell some clarity. There's the parts store I could get a wiper blade. No time now. Up another hill.

—Hey Karen! You home?

—No need to holler Bo I'm right here in the kitchen.

—Oh. Hi. I, uh, you want a beer, I brought a couple, I think they're still cold…

—I just poured a glass of wine, but go ahead, join me with your beer. How's the boat work?

—It's fine, um, well, Karen I think we should talk about, about er um—

—You're getting involved with someone aren't you Bo.

—Well I—what makes you say that?

—Oh, Bo. I love how you make me feel. But there was something going on last night…somehow I don't think it was about me.

Bo sighing. Face this sweet sad music.

—Hell. I guess I am. Maybe. I'm not sure where it's going. Or even if. But hurting you's the last thing I want to do.

—Come on Bo. We both know we don't go deep enough to be a lasting thing.

—Yeah…I suppose…how can you be so cool about it? You think it takes having a bunch of favors on someone for it to go deep?

—I'm not an expert. All I know is, during 18 years with Johnny I had more than enough favors and jealousy. Any more, I try to keep it simple.

—You do that, for sure. And sweet. But if we were to...ease off…does that make me staying here uncomfortable? Would you want me to move out?

—Let me think about it. You might consider your own comfort…it's not all that inconceivable I'll find someone else wants to play on my level.

—Wouldn't surprise me. But anyway, I'm going to be on the boat once the season starts, won't be much difference after next week…only thing is, moving my stuff out.

—There's no rush. Let's just see how it goes.

—I appreciate that. I'd better get back, crew showed up and is working unsupervised, who knows what bad habits she picked up over the winter.

—Okay then well…

—Well…

Gravitating together…can we risk a kiss yes.

—Just tell me one thing.

—Sure, what.

—Who is it.

—Oh, well, uh, her name's Myra. Works for the Watchdog. Just moved here a month or so ago.

—All right, then. If it was someone I knew, a friend, I'd be mad but, so...good fishing Bo.

—Okay Karen. See you then.

Bo taking the back road, glimpses between houses to the west of Mount Edgecumbe and its fading snow cap. Here is my estate with its economical motor home. Currently being enjoyed by a couple of Effie's chickens. Irregular tenants whose contributions have an unwholesome aura, could fix that jammed front window keep them out. But since they mostly take the front seat as their quarters and leave my rear berth alone, I may continue to embrace the concept of neighborly sharing. In homage to Karen's un-uptight approach to life. That was good, talking it out. Oh boy life is going to be a third less complicated. And maybe something will develop with Myra to supplant this painful residual Mariellousness, maybe I will become free to go in some better direction, maybe this is already true, after all the idea of going out tomorrow is getting exciting, yes this is cause for celebration and in just a while I will be in the Quixote, the perfect place for celebrating. Come on Bobcat let's go get ready.

No sign on the dock or back deck of carts groceries or gear.

—Hey Reilly what's happening! Oh there you are, wow, you got the windows resanded already?

—Almost. A few more to go.

—Well tear that sandpaper in half, I'll help you finish up. We should leave in half an hour.

Bo working on the galley window while Reilly finishes the last starboard front. Piratical black bandanna old jeans and a green tshirt. And, Bo notices for the first time, absence of bra, a new fashion statement about which I will not complain. Nipples moving in rhythm with her sanding, recollection of tapering breasts noted last summer during a mid August stop at the White Sulphur springs. Pragmatically, this doesn't bear too much thinking about. Bare thinking about.

—I'm about done here.

—Good, me too. If you'll wipe off the dust I'll sweep up. Then it'll be all ready to recoat in the morning. And we can get gone.

CHAPTER 14

The Quixote Club's lot a third full, sign on the door advertising tomorrow's Harlingen Night, special on tequila and Corona. Arguello occupying a table near the dart board's alcove, rapt in menu study. Bo stopping at the bar.

—Hi Herman. A pitcher over there where Wade is? And menus.

Bo and Reilly sliding in to the empty bench, Wade looking up.

—I consulted with Su Mi. She assures me this braised black cod with ginger soy glaze will be adequate to my needs.

Bo appropriating menu, scanning prices.

—Jesus. That'll teach me to make a hasty bet. But I'm surprised you aren't zeroing in on the king crab. According to price it'd be almost twice as adequate.

—Taken by itself, the dollar is not an absolute measure of anything. I suggest you order the king crab. Then to see whose was better, we'll arm wrestle.

—My mom taught me to never arm wrestle with

longliners. But here's our pitcher. Why don't we order, you know what you want Reilly?

—Salmon burger? Fries and salad. Hey, there's Neva! I better go catch up, scuse me guys.

—Pour a glass to take with you, this is going to disappear fast. I'll have the same, Herman. And I guess you know what Wade wants.

—Yes, the sablefish. Thanks Wade for not pretending to smoke tonight.

—Ah well. In deference to my dinner benefactor, I am posing as someone with a benevolent view of humanity. I don't think either of us brought a board, Bo, how about a game of darts.

—Yeah. Let me just poke my snout into this ale first—man! That's good. Life is getting gooder and gooder, Wade. 301?

—Sure, go ahead and start. So I understand you are throwing over the beautiful Karen for some non-Alaskan.

—What, are you following me around? How the hell do you know about that?

—Second page of the last Watchdog, you didn't see the headline? "Addled Troller Gives Up Perfect Relationship for Scrumptious Interloper".

—I think I can safely say the current staff would not print that story. Anyway you should get over this xenophobia, the only real Alaskans around here are Tlingits and you're not one.

—You dispute my claim of partial descendance from the Raven Clan?

—Ravin' lunatic is the closest you come, dude—

Fuck! That's two darts in a row bounced off the ring, what's going on?

—Viagra might help.

—Aww. I'm gonna refill this glass, that'll help. What's your score, I can't read it on the chalkboard.

—I haven't doubled in yet as you well know, asshole.

—Oh, yeah, that's too bad…man, that Hale's makes a good ale, I will say again.

—You ever try their Drawbridge? It tastes like they let a salmon swim around in it for a while. Intriguing, if kinda skanky.

—Yeah! I noticed the same thing. Only I thought it was more like a smoked salmon. An acquired taste, anyway. Look, here comes Herman, shall we postpone the game for a while? I'll help you remember your score. Hey, Reilly!

Herman distributing the salmon plates, promising to return with Arguello's. Reilly sliding in next to Wade.

—Neva's skipper was wondering if you think Salisbury'd be a good bet Tuesday, Bo.

—Oh brother.

—How'd this place get its name, anyway?

—Ha, that's a good question, you should ask Herman here.

—I don't want to talk about it. Your sablefish, here's silverware, anything else? Another pitcher?

—For sure, thanks Herman.

—He doesn't want to talk about it?

—Touchy subject. Let me get a bite or two of this

burger, kind of a long story, need the sustenance...omfa, ee fuh iffel eel uff mafeen uh iffover—

—There's no hurry, you can finish chewing.

—Mf. Okay. This place opened up around thirty years ago, named after the original Tlingit subgroup was here before the Russians showed up, part of the Raven clan which Wade claims partial descent from...hell, I don't know, maybe some wanderer did make it down to Portland and knocked up his great gramma—

—That's how our proud family lore has it—

—Anyway. They were called the Kiksadi, and this opened up as the Kiksadi Club. Popularity went up and down—it's pretty far out of town, so it has to have something going for it to attract customers, the way Herman's doing—and eventually it went belly up and sat vacant for a few years. Enter Herman, with a bunch of money he'd just come into and a hardon to find a bar and grill in Southeast. He does the whole deal over the phone. When the agent tells him the name, he thinks it's just an ignorant way of pronouncing Quixote. So when he's dealing with the Department of Licensing, he allows as how he'll keep the name for good luck and spells it out to them, and that becomes the spelling he has to put on his signage. Then he gets here and endures a raft of shit for the fuckup. Which I don't know, it's probably subsided after three years, but he's still sensitive as you can see.

Arguello augmenting the narrative.

—But so what? It's a perfectly good name either way. As I'm sure you know, Bo, Kiksadi means "original people" in Tlingit, can't go wrong with a native name, look at the Shee Atika, has the biggest clientele in Sitka. And most of the steady customers are fishermen. Given the vagaries of their profession, Cervantes' brand of blind optimism fits right in. The parallels are manifest. We're out there charging around, trying to slay demons and win romance, in conjuncture with our faithful (giving Reilly a sidearmed hug) if somewhat dimwitted sidekicks—

—Wait, what do you mean, faithful?

— Pulling it together even more, Raven himself was a totally quirky character, too. Really, it's the ideal appellation. Herman needs to get out of this defensive posture—Herman! The Quixote's a perfectly good name! Iberian pride!

Scattered hand claps from fans of Herman at nearby tables.

—Herman's from Boise.

—Okay, Bo. Better yet. Herman! Basque pride!

Applause spreading.

—His family came from south France, I think he told me.

—Herman! Buck up! Franco-Iberian sheepherder wino pride, goddamnit! Viva Alonso Quixano Don Quixote de la Mancha!

Widespread foot stomping, hollering of approval.

—You said it Wade!

—Listen to him, Herman!

Arguello energized, rising, fist in air

—Viva, viva el revolucion literario! Viva Cervantes y Garcia Lorca! Viva Perez Galdos! Rafael Alberti! Y Nicolas Guillen tambien, porque no?

Applause petering out. Rising discontent.

—What is that shit.

—Forget it Arguello.

—Yeah. Go back to Tijuana!

—We want Herman!

—Herman! Her-man! Her-man! Her-man! Her-man!

The chant spreading, stomping feet reverberating throughout the bar.

—Her-man! Her-man!

Himself coming out from behind the bar. Raising arms in benevolent gesture.

—Thank you! Thank you. And thank you Wade. All right I get it. I announce my new pride in the Club of Quixote!

—Hurray! You go Herman!

—In appreciation, I would like to offer a free beer—

—Whoooeee! Atta boy Herman! You the man!—

—With every order of the lobster-tenderloin dinner—

—No! Boooo!

— Traitorous!

—Go back to fuckin' Paris!

—And to further show my gratitude, here, Wade, is a dollar for the sound machine—

—No, worse yet—Noooo!

—Don't give it to Arguello! Anything but that!

Herman returning to bar. Arguello crossing to digital jukebox next to the bandstand, inserting coins, punching buttons. Mellow Paul Desmond sax pouring out into room.

—Aw, that's not so bad.

—At least it wasn't those god damn Goldberg variations again.

Gary entering the bar, approaching the table.

—Seem like you guys are enjoying yourselves.

—Gary! Have a seat. Have a beer! Have some of Wade's black cod.

—Sure, you might as well scavenge on my meal, these two haven't had any compunctions about it.

—Beer's good enough, I ate at home, I'll just grab a glass.

—I'll have another bite if he's not gonna.

—Me too, Wade?

—Parasitic Jaegers.

Gary filling a pint.

—So, if we survive this one day opening next Tuesday—

—Absolutely fucking ridiculous.

—what's the July 1 plan of attack?

—Well, you and I already talked about working toward the Grounds, and I've never known Wade to start anywhere else, so it sounds like we're in accord. How about radio channels?

—You guys still have those jailbreaked CBs?

—Yep.

—I haven't turned mine on since last fall but I assume it still works. Old things never seem to die.

—So how about that 28.650 frequency, upper for close range.

—That's fine here I'll write them down on this place mat.

—And, the big set?

—What was that eight megs we were on last year, 8923? Didn't seem like there was anyone else on there we were bothering.

—Sounds good, although I might listen around and see if there's another one, so we're not so predictable.

—This is all confidential, you understand Reilly?

—You bet. I promise I won't tell anyone. Unless the bidding gets to five figures. Mind if I go hang with Neva again?

—Go ahead on.

—Speaking of figures, she presents quite a nice one.

—I thought your tastes were more Rafaelesque, Wade.

—A lover of full-bodied Merlots can still find it easy to appreciate a tight little Chenin Blanc now and then.

—Something tells me this might be a time to ask how it's looking with Alsea fishing?

—For shit, in a word. I think she's going to flake on me. We got in a big yelling match on the phone, she took exception to my calling her a materialist cunt.

—How narrow minded of her.

—Heat of the moment, it slipped out. But oh

well. Signs have been growing that it's run its course. Anyway, you met my nephew Virgil last year, fished with me in September? I think he'll come this summer, he liked the money. I just gotta get him a set of headphones so I don't have to listen to that angry rap he plays. Assault on the senses. But he's a good worker.

—That's the important thing. How's the haulout going Gary?

—Smooth. Got the new zincs on, prop and bearing looked good. We'll touch up the bottom paint when they lift her in the morning and go back in the water. You got an ice appointment yet? Ours is Monday morning, nine.

—Shit, no. Damn! I better call Dave, like, now. You on the list, Wade?

— I stopped in at the ice house just before I came out here, there was only a couple of early slots left on Monday, six and six fifteen. Harbor's starting to fill up with the migrant fleet from down south. Fuckin' intruders.

—Says the guy originally from Oregon.

Gary taking empty pitcher to bar as Bo hauls cell from pocket and exits to parking lot. Returning some moments later.

—You had it right Wade the swarm is growing. Monday was gone, I had to settle for late Sunday night. But that's okay, I got good insulation. Gonna have to shovel it all out anyway before I get fresh ice for the real season. Which brings up the good news, Dave just opened up that list. I got 3:30 on

Wednesday, put you guys down for 3:45 and 4:00. You can call if you want to change.

—No that's perfect, thanks.

—Yep, works for me.

Bo refilling glass, drinking appreciatively

—All right. Good. Enough of this business then, on to the serious stuff: we got to finish our game, we got to drink this beer—

—Wait we should set up a calling schedule for the sideband, last year we checked in at 8:45 a.m. and p.m.—

—Yeah okay that's fine—

—but I think we were getting eavesdropped on. We should vary the time, say—

—Does anybody really know what time it is?

—how about 8:20 a.m. on even numbered days and—

—Does anybody really care?

—9:15 on the odds and—

—About time?

—then maybe the opposite for—

—If so I can't imagine why—okay! Fine! Whatever you think, just write it down on the place mat there. I got to go check out the player now, you got me thinking I need to hear some Chicago, nothing against your sweet sax man Wade but mellow's not making it.

Bo feeding quarters, standing back appreciatively as the percussive guitar starts

Bum bum bum bum *bum*

Bum bum bum bum *bum*
Bum bum bum bum *bum*
Bum bum bum
Bum bum bum

Hip moving reflexively as tight brass section comes in setting up the solo vocal. Who is this tugging on my sleeve, Reilly.

—This is hot Bo let's dance.

—Yeah it is…dance? Us? Well sure why not.

Bo channeling the beat, various limbs jerking in reasonably close time with the rhythm. Reilly laughing, circling him in modified hopscotch routine. Occasionally pausing to wag hips in manner appreciated by onlookers. Some couples of whom rise and join in general goofiness. Growing even goofier as the brass bridge segues in to wa wa

chu-chu chu-chu wow wow
chu-chu chu-chu wag wag
chu-chu chu-chu wow wow wag wag wag wag

—I don't know Wade. Seems like a contest to see who can make the biggest fool of themself.

—Ah, have another beer Gary. Dance now, for tomorrow we die. Or fish. Or cut bait. Or how the fuckever it goes. Why don't you take Bo's turn on the dart board, get this game going again.

—Dance now with whoever works a little better if you're not married.

—There was a fellow drove around Fairbanks for

a while with a bumper sticker on his truck said 'Married but not dead.'

—That's sounds like a dumb way to lay a zinger on the wife.

—Now I think about it, the driver and his sticker weren't on the scene very long.

—Probably moved back to Fort Worth, got a new sticker, 'Single but not solvent'.

—Tell me about it. The perils of navigating the straits of marriage are not to be taken lightly, I can say as a three trip veteran.

—Yeah well, seemed to get easier once I gave up the idea of being in charge when I'm off the boat. Not to mention the pursuit of happiness in other quarters. Weird, isn't it? There's something about being with only one person doesn't feel right, but you spread yourself around and it's a world of hurt.

—We could blame Adam and Eve for the incongruity.

—Yeah? How's that?

—An anthro-archaeologists' theory. Eating the apple and getting kicked out of the garden was an allegory for when we gave up hunting and gathering, and took up agriculture. A big screwup, it turned out, farming was way more tedious and took a whole lot more time and effort than browsing. Skeletons of the agricultural types are much more worn down than the hunters. Anyway, whereas before everyone was kind of a free agent, now some developed into farm bosses to keep the workers toiling away. The bosses needed order and structure to keep control, and decided fidelity was more orderly than the polygamy which had been prevalent before.

—Wow, who knew…I wonder…you think that because us fishermen're more like hunter gatherers, we're more in touch with our adulterous roots? More likely to have the roving eye than the guy growing potatoes in eastern Oregon?

—Could be. But I think the wider society's more aligned with the potato farmer. Serial monogamy's the only answer I've found, and it's still not much of one. Seems like if a woman's happy inside she'll forgive a lot. If not, she'll be on you for any little thing. You tried to keep two happy for a while, didn't I hear?

— Well yeah, back when I was idealistic about almost everything I thought if you just followed your heart, everything would fall into place. But, instead of a cozy triangle it turned out to be just sharp corners. Fishing got to be like a vacation from it all. Finally they both dumped me. So then I moved into this free love commune on the upper Rogue.

—That worked?

—Seemed kinda exciting for a while, but...I was seriously tripping on mushrooms and acid…let the boat go downhill…maybe I was setting myself up for what happened, I don't know.

—You mean when you lost the first Antigone there off Newport?

—Yeah.

Silence descending, the two friends contemplating the fear all mariners hold in the back of their minds.

Wade familiar with the story—Gary taking a chance with his small troller fishing fifty miles out on the albacore grounds, rough windy night, a steep following sea engulfing the stern and flooding through the open fish hatch and wheelhouse door, time only for a brief Mayday before jumping off the sinking boat. Eerie sight of the still-burning nav lights disappearing below, and then blackness. Gary trying to hold on to the wave-tossed floating hatch cover, bruised and battered and rapidly weakening until in a thousand to one chance, Matt on the Loran who'd noted his Mayday position and steamed toward it spotlights him among the dark seas.

—Worst thing ever happened to me, and the luckiest, at the same time. After that I thought, time to get your shit together.

—That's when you met Julie?

—No, she was one of the two from earlier. I guess I always knew she was the one. After busting my ass getting the money together for a new boat, I dedicated myself to getting her back.

—Success on all fronts, huh. Julie's a fine woman, the Antigone II's a serious fishing machine. All tricked out—I'm surprised you don't ditch us old-schoolers and partner up with a real fish-killer fleet like the Breeze's.

—Aw, those guys. Sure, everybody'd like to catch more fish…I like good equipment, but they're a little over the top.

—A little, you think? Side scanning sonar? Software to create your own 3D bottom charts?

Underwater video cams so you can change your lures to match the bait that's down there? What happens if everyone ramps up to that level? The fish get caught sooner, season's shortened, anyone who wants to fish at a reasonable pace loses out.

—Yeah, sure...well anyway, you and Bo are a lot more fun to listen to on the radio. I better get on home, Wade, I'll see you later.

Red-faced Bo and Reilly rejoining, pouring remnants of Gary's pitcher into glasses. Bo doubletaking at the chalkboard.

—What the fuck? You're ready to double out and I'm still at 235? Some inept person has been darting on my board. Said the papa bear.

CHAPTER 15

Bo pondering on drive back to town a not so subtle shift in attitude coming from deckhand. Illustrated now by her position on bench seat, not overtly close but not over by passenger window either, some animal heat transmitting my way. Maybe best to take this bull by the horns, wait bad metaphor. Cow by udder? Worse…engage colleague in friendly dialogue.

—That was fun huh, dancing and all.

—For sure! Is all of Chicago's music that good?

—A lot of it, yeah. I've got a few of their albums I got off my folks' collection, you can check out…look Reilly, something feels a little different this year…we've got a long season ahead, good to be on the same page, you want to talk about it?

Reilly staring through windshield, face momentarily pensive in dashboard light, before relaxing, leaning back against door and facing Bo with knee lifted onto seat.

—Sure. It's—I guess maybe I'm practicing? Things in Arizona are kinda, changed.

—Practicing? Changed?

—Yeah…Max and I…well, it's kind of in limbo right now. We've been on this straight line track for, forever it seems. Everything all planned out. He'll finish his master's next year, we'll get married in the summer, he'll get a job, I'll finish my degree the year after, start work myself, then begin thinking about kids. It's like I could look ahead and see exactly how my life was going to go. But this spring, I don't know, I just started thinking I needed to be more spontaneous, like maybe there was a lot more out there I wasn't getting.

—There's a lot out there for sure, but sometimes you need some kind of framework.

—Okay, I'm not talking about turning it into a dice game. I know I'm going to be teaching once I finish school, but how I get there, and where it might happen, it feels like it'd be nice to leave some of it up to chance. And Max is just so certain about everything. It's like it's totally predictable: he'll be working in solar in the Bay Area where he's comfortable. Two years from now in March we'll have a baby and it'll probably be a boy. A year and a half later we'll have a girl. We'll drive a Honda, something that acts like a minivan but looks a little cooler. On Tuesday evenings he'll watch the kids so I can go to my book group. We'll have some trendy sitcom we'll watch at 9:30 every Thursday! It's like, I've already lived the next ten years of my life!

—Doesn't sound like all that bad a life.

—Oh, I know, but—anyway it just got to seem

like too much. So before I left, I said I thought we should back off for a while with the plans.

—And he was cool with that?

—Yeah, I think so. You know, I was clear, I didn't want to end it, at all, I just thought we could use some perspective.

—And perspective, then, means…practicing? With other guys?

—Well, I don't know. I mean maybe…or not…anyway, if I've seemed sort of, flirty, with you, I guess I'm just trying it out, because I can, because you're safe.

—Not sure if I want to be the kind of guy women think of as safe.

—You know what I mean, you're respectful. I don't have to worry about you taking advantage?

—Ha. Well as long as it's helping your perspective. Anyway, here we are. I'm going to go swing by the Lakeside. Tomorrow let's start by replacing the trolling wire, then when it warms up get the final coats on the trim, rainex the windows, organize the fishing gear. It'll be a full day.

—I'll be ready. That was great tonight Bo, thanks.

Scooting over and planting an exuberant kiss on Bo's cheek before climbing out. Bo watching her cross the parking lot before disappearing down the gangplank, steeply angled now at low tide. Even though last year convinced me the employer-employee relationship was the best, can't help thinking Wade's right, an attractive woman is the ultimate work of art. The sensuous movement of hips viewed from behind as she walks…if I was given to self-analysis I would be wondering what it means being so attracted to women who are walking away. Like Mariella…oh no I'm not gonna start feeling sorry for myself again now, am I? Jesus, life just won't ever stay simple. If it wasn't for Myra, I'd be totally confused trying to figure this riddle out.

Now I'm just partly confused.

CHAPTER 16

Next evening, a cleaned up Bo u-turning at the end of Seward to pull in next to curb. Scrutinizing the building. Kind of a dump, this? Two story flat roof, gray paint peeling off old siding strakes. Different story inside the outer door though, clean, broad steps with a polished wood banister leading up to a three sided landing. Here's 2B on the west side. Press the doorbell…no footsteps audible, maybe I can see through this peephole. Leaning to press eye against the tiny circle of glass, stumbling in and colliding with occupant as she opens the door abruptly.

—Oops. Hi there Myra.

—Hi, Bo. Would you like to come in?

—Sure—wow, this is a nice place—

Green and blue oriental rug on gleaming hardwood, oak, looks like. Evening light between gathered curtains on broad west-facing window, view over the Pioneer Home's roof, tops of masts in ANB Harbor, a few slivers of the Sound visible between buildings on Japonski. Cinnamon smoke drifting up from a stick poked through an aperture in what looks like a cat skull on fireplace mantel. And Myra. Jeans again, dark V neck sweater, hair clasped into two strands falling over shoulders. These green eyes looking up.

—Are we in a hurry? Or do you want a beer?

—Beer would be great, but…I got a reservation at Ludvig's for 7:30, what time is it, twenty after, if you're okay with eating there I suppose we should go. I was lucky to get in, they had a cancellation.

—Sure, let's go. I'll just get my jacket.

Truck doors closing nearly simultaneously, Myra sliding over close. If compatibility was measured as inverse function of separation distance on bench seats we'd be pretty high on the scale here. Set in second gear, Myra taking Bo's offered hand and pulling it down to rest on soft thigh. Bo expending considerable effort steering one-armed without disturbing this arrangement. Disengaging at parking spot on Katlian.

—This is great, I've heard about this place. I guess we could have walked, huh.

—Yeah. But it might rain. Ha ha I said 'might'. Must have forgotten where we are. You know how much rainfall you're gonna get here in Sitka?

—More than Idaho?

Pushing door open into this warm close space.

—If 86 inches is more than Idaho.

Directed to a small table made intimate by candles and a colored glass lamp on the wall above. Jackets on chair backs, settling in.

—86! Where I grew up it was about 25. Maybe I should buy an umbrella.

—Sure, you don't mind getting laughed at. It's a matter of pride to ignore the rain here, people might get sort of, derisive. But hell, nobody will even notice if you're using an umbrella in the winter, cause it's so dark you can hardly see anything at all for about three months.

—Sooo…now I don't know whether to get an anti-depression light box, or save the trouble and just shoot myself.

—No, don't do that. Look on the bright side. You could've ended up in Ketchikan. They get 160 inches a year, there—

Risk of spiral into meteorological depression eased as waitress appears to distribute menus and wine list.

—Think we can take care of a bottle of wine with dinner?

—Sure. Can I vote for a red?

—My preference too—although it might violate the whites with seafood regulation, depending on what we order, but we could be scofflaws, let's see what's on the list here, Pinot, Cabernet, Merlot, other reds—holy shit, they've got a—

Barolo jumping off the page, jolting a memory surge, Bo's mind veering ten thousand miles to the east—

—What, they've got a what?

—Sorry…a Barolo, they have, it's a really good rich Italian, we could try it…I'm looking at the paella, which it's got chorizo in it, so maybe I wouldn't have to go to jail for putting a red together with fish…

—This Caesar salad looks good to me, and its scallops are wrapped in bacon.

The bottle ordered and served swirling into glasses, liquid sunset color melding with the orange in the walls' Mediterranean décor. Glass touching glass in a wordless toast. Here's to the possibility of new memories to overlay…the Mediterranean…Bo's gaze straying helplessly toward anomalous evening sunlight coming through curtained window seeing not the sparse traffic on Katlian but big swells shouldering in from a storm in the western Med, crashing spectacularly on the rocks below the rented room in Manarola, the same evening sun that had burnished Mariella's hair as they passed out from under the hillside olive grove's shade her beauty stunning him so he had to pull her back and close and inhale deep the clean warm female smell of her—damn me for choosing this damn Ludvig's, should have gone to the Shee Atika with its siliconed presentation and its hard edged vibe. The only memories there of ridiculous drunken efforts to postpone the end of already foundered nights —

—Bo are you all right?

Not good to disregard partner, fool, get back in the moment, maybe this excellent wine will help.

—Sorry. Every once in a while I get a little spacey but it's no reflection on the company. I don't think I've said how nice you look tonight.

—Well gee I guess I can handle being ignored a

little if it produces compliments. Whether or not they're flattery.

—Absolutely not I mean it.

The Barolo's rich warmth spreading outward from tongue and throat, Bo regaining balance.

—So, how do you like Sitka so—

—So how did you get into—

Exchange of grins, Myra resuming first.

—Into salmon fishing? Was it in your family?

—Oh. Nope. Happened sort of by accident. I mean, I knew what fishing was about, growing up in Juneau you can hardly miss it. But I never even thought about doing it myself until I was at the U of A in Fairbanks. I met this premed student who trolled in the summer, we got to be pretty good friends and I went out on a trip with him one July. It was the coolest thing I'd ever done, and I couldn't think about anything else but getting my own boat. Twelve years now and there's nothing I'd rather be doing.

—Not many can say that. You're a lucky man.

—Yeah. Or else I've got a stunted view of what everybody else is doing.

—I don't think so. From what I've seen so far, and from talking to Julie, it seems like a really cool life style.

—Well, she's a pretty creditable source, fished with Gary for five years, before they had kids.

—She makes it sound like something I'd really like to try…sometime…

Talk slowing as food arrives. The deep pleasure of

a well cooked savory meal. How clever of me to order a dish of Spanish origin and not Italian, and not have to fight distraction from that quarter as well as the wine…

—And anyway, Barolo's not from anywhere near Florence.

—What?

Oops did I say that out loud?

—Uh, I mean that drinking this Italian wine with paella, which came out of Spain, isn't any weirder than with some dish from Tuscany? Because Barolo is way up in the northwest part of Italy, by the French border?

—Oh, I, think I get it…maybe...where's Caesar salad from? I wouldn't want the wine to clash with it because it's really, really good.

—Yeah! Everything here is, the owner's way into flavor blending. It's like she's playing your sense of taste as if it was a violin. I think Caesar salad was invented in Tijuana. But, what were we talking about?

—Tijuana that's funny ha ha. Fishing, it was. Is your friend still doing it?

—Yep. Made it through school, now he's an emergency room doc. It being a high-turnover front line kind of position, they give him summers off to keep him happy, and he goes trolling. Pretty good balance, really, operate on people in the winter, and on fish in the summer. I think his mortality rate is a little better in the winter.

—One would hope.

—So what was it brought you to Sitka?

—Well, I already told you, that night at the Quixote Club, but I guess I shouldn't expect you to remember. You seemed like you might have been getting close to your alcohol capacity.

—Um. Yes. Well…I guess I recall you said something about it just before you rushed off to some hot assignation at the Shee Atika.

—Oh, that was hot all right. I was meeting Julie to return the car she'd loaned me so I could look around. Anyway, I'll give you the short version…again…maybe you'd like to take notes this time?

—I'll practice some mnemonics.

—Okay. Graduated from Boise State, worked at some not very exciting jobs for a few years, got to thinking I wanted to try living near the water, saw an ad for a reporter at the Watchdog and here I am.

—Okay, George Washington the Third.

—Huh?

—For GW3, graduated, work, water, Watchdog. Gives me a framework of how your life went since college. Which I could fill in with more details…if we get to know each other better.

—It'd be all right with me if that happened.

Her sweet smile

—Well, me too…I mean, I had an idea it might, after the way you threw yourself at me in the back of Gary's truck.

And her laughing eyes

—Why Bo I think it would be just as reasonable to say you became rather aggressively intimate there…

Gleaming in the candle light

…not that I'm complaining.

—Me neither.

The three feet of intervening table beginning to seem inordinately wide.

—Looks like this bottle's about gone, shall we get another, you want some dessert?

—We could do that, or…I've got some Cointreau back at my place, we could try?

—What a nice idea.

Last swallows taken, check paid, out onto the sidewalk Bo leaning against the building and pulling her close finding her willing mouth this first kiss so sweet your lips your breath your body against mine

—I don't want to move.

—No.

—But I guess we could maybe there'll be another opportunity.

—Yes.

The ride uphill wordless, bodies at 10 on proximity. Again up the stairs, Myra opening the door into the now dark apartment with residual scent of cinnamon, handing bottle and two shot glasses to Bo, relighting candles and crossing to stereo. Returning to take glass and lean close, sweet orange bite on the tongue and the low tones, slow harmonies of Haden and Metheny guitar and bass. Spontaneous movement toward bedroom's open door inside which Myra lights two more candles. Bo noting handsewn quilt on double bed before she moves back close and it becomes impossible to notice anything beyond this curve of neck to which my lips are irresistibly drawn. Allow me to lift this sweater and yes unclasp that while I take off my shirt, the wonder of breasts first exposed in brave vulnerability oh yes let's remove these other fabric impediments and climb beneath the covers to lie skin on skin temple to temple and let our bodies move slowly through the quiet rapture woven in this achingly beautiful music until we tumble together into sweet oblivion oh God you feel good....

Bo rolling a quarter turn to take weight off, holding on tight to keep bodies joined for at least a while longer during the slide toward sleep. Some hours later waking to brief disorientation in strange bed before remembering. Myra curled close, Bo leaning over to place soft kiss on hair before lying contentedly back. Maybe there is hope for me yet.

CHAPTER 17

A low pressure trough stalls just south of Kodiak Island. An associated weather front crosses northern area waters this afternoon. Area forecast for the waters from Cape Decision to Cape Edgecumbe including Sitka Sound: small craft advisory. Tonight, southeast winds 20 to 25 knots with higher gusts, seas to six feet. Tuesday wind veering to southwest 20 to 25, seas building to eight feet. Tuesday night—

Bo switching off the VHF.

—Phooey. Crummy weather for a crummy opening, at least it's consistent. But what the fuck we might as well go see what it looks like. Why don't you get the lines off. You need to get a coat?

—I'm good. It's not raining that hard.

Bo waiting on stern until Reilly looses the bowline leaving half a turn. Flipping the stern line off the dock cleat and bringing it inboard, ducking into pilot house to helm. Thumbs up through the window, reversing hard after Reilly pulls the bow line free. Coasting into fairway and shifting into forward toward gap in jetty. Bo slowing to let a bright blue double-ender go through the entrance. Nice new coat of paint Ralph's got on the Nina. Looks like he's going to go up channel toward Salisbury. How many others heading that way, one two three…wow that's 18 just in view.

Reilly taking a position near pilot seat and peering ahead, shoulders of sweatshirt water darkened and hair wet on forehead.

—Maybe it was raining that hard after all. Where we going? Looks like a pilgrimage.

—Yeah, I think everyone else listened to the weather, Salisbury'll give the most protection from this blow. Or maybe they're all still thinking about my sea pooey.

—Sea pooey?

—Ah, it's a long stupid story. Anyway, I think we'll head west. Take the wheel here will you, I'm going to lower the poles.

The wind light in this protected end of the Sound but vestigial swells frothing the rocks and islets south of the runway on Japonski and lifting the Walter's bow, Bo having to time the poles' release to keep them from crashing back up into the crosstree. Reentering the cabin to hang damp watch cap by the stove and lay a course on the plotter past Vitskari Rocks. Progress toward which accompanied by freshening breeze and visibility dropping, until the buoy at Kulichkof shows only as an intermittent smudge on the radar a mile to windward. Wind waves transforming from small hull-slappers to sharp whitecapped four-footers that crash against the

Walter's side, bursts of spray spattering the port windows. Two succeeding seas delivering a one two punch that lurches the boat sharply to starboard. Kettle sliding across stove to bang against rail burping a slosh of boiling water onto floor. Bo cutting the throttle.

—Okay okay, time for the port stabilizer. You want to put it in, or shall—

Reilly already disappearing out the back door. Rattle of chain being freed, muted splash as the weighted fin dives and swings out to hang from pole. Immediate reduction in roll. Reilly reappearing.

—No flies on you.

—I was motivated. Nine months since I was on the ocean, I'm having a little readjustment issue.

—You want an ear patch? I've got a couple leftovers.

—No I'll be fine, I'll just curl up here on the settee. Let me know if you need something.

Bo resuming speed, autopilot holding a course just south of west. The ride for a time more stable but just as wet, heavy flights of spray hitting the cabin side and flying past the windows from left to right. Past the Vasilief Bank, seas rising further as the wind's unobstructed fetch doubles, the Walter now rolling heavily to port off the back sides of the waves. Bo grabbing the wheel to keep from catapulting off the pilot seat as a particularly steep sea wheels the rail well down allowing the next wave to crash on board. Kettle sliding the other way and slopping another gout onto the stove top. Ensuing sizzle and cloud of steam. Bo pulling oilskin out of hanging locker. Hollering as he exits out the back door.

—Get the clamps on that damn kettle, will you.

Bo throwing the starboard stabilizer in, then gazing aft to the east where Sitka has disappeared in cloud—shit! I forgot to call Myra! What a doofus…reentering the cabin to hang up streaming coat and grab phone. No service, damn. Well we'll be back in tomorrow night.

Wedging back into pilot seat against further ejection and beginning a grumbling internal indictment of the situation. Couldn't the weather service have overestimated the wind for a change? No, they persist in their callously accurate forecasting. Prospects for this opening being anything other than an ordeal diminish hourly and I might ask myself why am I struggling to get out here when it's probably going to be even rougher tomorrow and we will not catch squat. Not that going to Salisbury would've been any better. Sure it's protected but it'll be impossible to find even a modest piece of real estate to fish on up there with fifty or more boats crammed into the open sector.

But what good is that comparison. Lethal injection may be better than hanging, but why choose either if you have something better to do. Like, I could be cosily esconced at the Quixote now with a tall cool glass considering which of Su Mi's excellent dinner dishes to select and preparing to waste Arguello at cribbage—although I've never known him to miss a chance to fish. I wonder which way he went. If he's on this end I could get him on the CB but maybe I'll wait until after I get out here and look at the feed situation. Let's see I won't be able to drive over that trench out in the middle without turning upwind and suffering even more, but if I hold this course I can swing past those humps between there and Lazaria. Then on the way in to the anchorage it'll be mostly on the stern so that's good. And another good thing, this is breaking Reilly in so she won't be green for July first when it's all for real, so...so I've somehow warped myself into an optimistic frame of mind. Which could be disturbing but with luck it'll turn out to be only a temporary condition.

With both stabilizers in, Walter K of deep sea kindly hull settling into the ride. Bo getting comfortable in pilot seat, keeping partial attention on radar and sounder but otherwise letting cabin warmth and humming engine work their tranquilizing effect. Time slipping by...ha, there's a feedball on the sounder. Nothing spectacular, but looks like there's enough here and there some fish could be making a living, hopefully king salmon. Okay here we are, if I come around gradually it'll take us right in to the anchorage behind Lazaria where we can get out of this slop.

Bo coasting around the east end of the high rocky grass-and spruce-topped double island. Three boats visible in the good holding ground tight up against the cliff face on the north corner, a couple others anchored in deeper water outside. Bo idling in to a spot farther east just outside the kelp beds. Reilly stepping outside to undog the winch and at Bo's signal freewheel the anchor to clatter downward. Eerie clank as the anchor hits bottom, Bo backing down and digging the flukes in. There we are. Not the smoothest spot but way better than where we just were.

Reilly climbing into fish hold and emerging with bag of food, grabbing a railing as the boat rolls in remnant chop coming around the island's south side. Hanging oilskins in locker, gazing wistfully at other boats.

—I guess we'd lose our edge if we slept in that calm water?

—Nothing against calm, but the only room left over there is on the outside. When the west swell comes up in the night we'll be in the better spot. I'm going to see if I can reach Wade.

Bo switching on a clunky retro chrome-faced CB mounted on ceiling, considering with microphone in hand before pressing the transmit button.

—Hello Wade, you pick me up here? Hello Wade? How about you Gary?

Ten seconds of silence.

—Pick me up Wade? Hello hello?

—Okay, I got you Bo. I was just climbing into the skiff to go in for a soak. This shitty weather's not good for anything else, I figure.

—What! You're at the springs? Damn, that was

smart. How come I'm not there?

—*Inferior genetic makeup? Or poor nurturing during childhood, I don't know. You must be across the way if I can hear you this well.*

—Yeah, I guess we'll see if we can struggle out and try the high spots in the morning. There was a little feed showing, but nothing great. Did you check over there on your way out?

—*Nope. Came straight here on the inside. I'm still so pissed about them making us fish this stupid opening, I'm imposing a ban on personal suffering for the period. If I miss anything, you masochists can have my share.*

—That doesn't sound like you. This the first indication of a new benevolent Arguello?

—*Don't get your hopes up. Near term, though, I'm going to be a lot more benevolent after half an hour or so in this hot water. Gotta go, man. I'll check with you in the morning.*

—Okay Wade. No word from Gary, so I guess he's in the other spot with the crowd. Good soaking there. Check you tomorrow.

CHAPTER 18

Bo rising toward consciousness dimly aware the buzzer has been going off for a long time. Swinging legs off bunk and looking out into a dim gray world. The Walter's bow facing west and into the swell coming around the island, gentle pitching, no roll. The ultimate soporific motion but I need to get moving. Socks, pants, boots. Sweatshirt. Position kettle over firebox and turn up the carburetor. Engine room next.

Hold on—I'm Cummins
Hold on—I'm Cummins
Well don't you ever
Feel sad

Okay oil and water good, let's fire up.

The chain crawling over the roller and onto the winch, Bo assessing the other end of the anchorage. Yep those outside guys are rolling pretty good in the swell now. This wind feels just like the forecast said, i.e. shitty. Can't tell for sure here in the lee, though.

Only one way to find out. Better mix myself a cup of instant coffee and cocoa first, keep me going till Reilly gets up and makes a pot of the good stuff.

Bo backing away from the kelp and skirting an invisible underwater rock before angling toward open water. Light growing with approach of sunrise, horizon now visible as a ragged heaving line. That's not good, the horizon's supposed to be flat. I guess we're in for it. Here we go, out of the lee. Shit! These things are every bit of eight feet. Okay Walter it's up to you now.

Steep, short period seas in various shapes approaching from the right to take the Walter broadside. The sharper ones, tops collapsing, presenting walls that shove the boat up and to the left before slipping below, leaving a void. Ensuing violent roll to windward and the next wave heaving up.

Reilly appearing at top of companionway, carefully navigating from one handhold to the next.

—Morning there. You're up early.

—It's like a rock tumbler down there, I was afraid I'd lose all my skin rolling up and down the cabin walls.

—Not the best ride, that's for sure. But another ten minutes I can slow down and put the gear in, should be a little better.

—Maybe I'll wait till then to make the coffee.

The Walter circusing on to the southeast, yaw pitch and crazy roll. Broken clouds wheeling overhead with occasional light gaps offering false hope of respite. Here, this is close enough.

Cutting throttle to 800 rpms, pulling on full raingear and exiting to unlash and stow trolling hatch covers and climb in the cockpit. The stacked gear having slopped around on the way out requiring tedious untangling of leaders. Try twenty-five fathoms of wire to start, that way I can troll close to those humps without snagging bottom. With the wind blowing us sideways like this, good chance of tangling…lower the windward float line first, then the port float, then the deeps. Okay fish, I'm ready if you are. You'll have to be pretty agile, the way the gear's jerking around. Hello? Hello? Anyone down there listening? I wonder if that coffee's ready.

Bo grabbing knotted rope hanging from boom and hauling himself up and out of the pit just as a breaking wave smacks the quarter and sloshes thirty gallons of seawater into his just vacated space. That was lucky. Quick hop up here between rolls to the fish hatch, hold on till the next pause and scuttle forward to the cabin door through which I believe I detect a French roast aroma—what's that a fish?

Bell on the starboard pole tip tugging urgently. Oh boy, something to look forward to.

—Hey Reilly do I smell what I think I smell?

— Thermos is in the sink. If we're going to fish this kind of weather a lot, you might get one of those galley harnesses they use on sailboats so you can belt yourself in and not go flying across the cabin.

—I need to get a mug before I can think about boat improvements.

Bo wedging into pilot seat and scrutinizing depth sounder. Not very damn much besides interference, what with the boat thrashing around. Quarter mile more and we can turn east around the 14-fathom pinnacle and head downwind, that'll give any fish collected there a chance to jump on. Plus it'll be a lot smoother ride for the first run-through. Or less unpleasant let's say. Oof, Jesus that was a violent one.

Several minutes later Bo cutting pilot and making wide careful turn to new course east northeast. Slowing engine to low idle and retracing the back deck obstacle course. Much less perilous now with seas on stern. Starting the port float line up. Jesus it's coming in slow. Could play a game of cribbage waiting for the float to crawl up to the boat. But here it is, flailing elusively in the wind—got it. Okay come on fish.

Hanging the first empty spoon on the standby line. And the second. And the top flasher. And the next, damn, what happened to that ringer? Aha must be on this bottom spread, line's dragging way back—shit!

Grabbing the leader and hauling in a huge mottled brown ling cod, its big toothy mouth gaping wide open and dragging like a towed bucket. God damn it what are you doing on here you know you're not in season. You and your bony jaw which of course won't want to give up the hook. Oh well, I suppose you aren't any happier about this than I am.

Bo bracing knees and leaning outboard, hauling

the big fish up. Working gaff into curve of hook and jerking violently upward, successful on third try. Fish flopping back into the sea, shaking its head like a dazed boxer before slanting down into the dark.

Bo pulling a remnant piece of cartilage off the hook before tossing it out and starting the wire down. That sucks. But he'd been on for a while, maybe he scared the salmon away from that line and they're all on the others. Speaking of which, isn't that a fish biting on the starboard deep which I'm about to pull? Going this direction I can read the bells better and I believe I can say with some certainty that is a member of the onchorynchus species and not some god damn bottom fish.

Optimism born out, the deep line yielding one 20-pound king salmon. Well that's something anyway.

—Hey Reilly! Got some business for you.

Bo shifting to port side and winding in deep line as Reilly turns on deck hose climbs into starboard hatch and begins dressing. The deep producing a 9-pound feeder king and a small rockfish.

—Well I guess I've seen better production.

—Yeah, how come you had your gigantic trip just before I got here.

—Wasn't my plan, it would've been even giganticker if you'd been here to help, but no, you were stubbornly immersed your philosophy study in Arizona.

—Well, someone's got to get educated and bring some enlightenment to this mass of obtuseness you call a state.

—What is with everyone associating me with that word? Even if only through proximity—what, just because we think that the universe is only 6,000 years old? And that you should have a kid every time you make love? And there should be an assault rifle in every closet? And that homosexuals are mentally ill? You think that makes us obtuse?

—Definitely yeah, I—

Bo warned by loud familiar hissing, grabbing Reilly's arm and ducking as a wave rushes up and breaks on the transom. Its top flung forward over cockpit, filling checkers. Crouched figures straightening, looking at each other. Water sluicing down Reilly's face into collar from soaked hair.

—You should keep your hood up Reilly.

What could be the hint of a grin.

—Thanks Bo I know I can always count on you for good advice.

Bo resetting the deep line before stepping into cabin to check position on plotter. God damn this wind is zooming us along, three knots, three point two, almost too fast for kings. Ten minutes and we'll already be at the east end of this drag where I saw that feed on the sounder yesterday. Make a pass through there before turning around, I can run the lines on the uphill tack. Might as well stay inside here. Hollering from the back deck.

—Hey Bo this fish is a quarter inch short, even if I stretch the tail.

—What? Damn. Well it's dead, isn't it. Might as well save it to eat.

Small red icon crawling up plotter screen, sounder blue and blank. Bo reaching up to punch the WX button on the VHF, enduring the other area forecasts until Sitka Sound comes up.

—Today, winds southwest 25 to 30 knots, seas to 9 feet. Tonight, southwest winds switching to west and diminishing after midnight—

Bo switching back to channel 16. This just sucks. Conditions are barely fishable, forecast is shitty, and I have one and a half fish for almost two hours. But maybe this hump that we're just now passing will produce something. I'm going to continue with my plan because I can think of no other thing to do except perhaps go back to school and become an actuary. What's that sound.

Reaching the door in three quick steps, Bo craning up at pole tips. Three of four bells ringing. Ah sweet music. That's more like it. Go back in and put mark on the plotter, troll just a little farther and give the lines a chance to fill up before turning back. Okay this is good enough.

—Hey Reilly I'm turning around here it's going to get bouncy!

Revving the engine through the turn. Bet I'll have to get up to near running speed to keep the gear working while we beat upwind. Shit, this is going to be awful.

The Walter struggling up steep wave faces, plunging violently down into succeeding troughs.

Progress sometimes entirely stalled by the steep oncoming walls of water. Spray blooming off the bow, filling air to both sides of boat as the wind sweeps it aft.

Buoyed by expectation, Bo jumping down into cockpit and starting starboard line in, peering down expectantly as the first snap appears, its leader stretched back and twitching, yes a fish on the top spread wait—shit it's a coho.

Letting the line continue spooling in, Bo quickly hauling leader and lifting the small silver wriggling fish, flipping hook out of mouth with gaff as the next spread appears similarly loaded. And the next. And the one below that, all bearing silvers except the lead spoon on which a tiny chilipepper rockfish trails. Fifty-pound cannonball swinging in small arcs just below the block, Bo balefully eying the bright orange fish, its eyes bugged out, swim bladder exploded out of mouth from the abrupt pressure change. Fuck a duck. This is worse than catching nothing, loading up on these coho a week before I can keep them.

—Well then Bo…doing there?

Arguello's voice wind-torn as it emits from back deck speaker, pulling Bo out of grim reverie. Lowering lead into holder on rail before lurching into the cabin.

—That you Wade?

— Yes, it is I. Are you fishing, or putting the finishing

touches on your omelet?

—I wish it was breakfast I was into instead of this world of hurt. Yeah I'm fishing. Or pretending to. I've got two kings and the lines are filled with silvers and the weather is absolutely for shit but other than that. . .other than that it's still all fucked up.

—*You sound morose. It might improve your spirits to try over here.*

—Really? You find something? It's not rough?

—*We're mostly in the lee here east of the island. Turning around where it starts to get rough on the north end. Got about twenty now.*

—Jesus. That makes my morning...kinda. Thanks Wade. Probably see you after a bit.

—*Morning there.*

Bo jumping down into pit and starting float line in. Reilly joining after dropping cleaned salmon into fish hold.

—We're going to charge over to Biorka once I get the gear in. Why don't you start pulling that side?

Lines coming in fast now with engine at high speed, the pair shaking off silver after silver, dancing to keep balance on the leaping and plunging cockpit floor. Bo climbing out as Reilly nears the end of her last line.

—Put the floats down in here and lash the covers on when you're done, okay? Could be a little lumpy going across.

Bo laying a line on the plotter to his guess at Wade's position, then waiting until he sees Reilly securing cockpit covers. Increasing RPMs to running speed. The Walter pursuing some depraved dream of glory as a rodeo bull, managing to maniacally pitch and roll at the same time. Bo watching speed over ground readout on plotter with disapproval. Well this may be an awful ride but at least it's slow. We're barely doing two and a half knots. Holy shit!

Lethal streak of galvanized steel flying past the window as a monster roll pulls the starboard stabilizer out of a wave trough, the thirty pound triangle zooming forward to jerk at end of chain tether and splash back into the next wave, just off the bow.

That could be dangerous.

Bo laying new route and adjusting course to take weather on stern quarter. Cessation of pitching, roll not much reduced but smoother and slower. Reilly hanging raincoat in locker.

—I filleted that chili pepper to go with eggs for breakfast, in case it ever becomes cookable in here.

—It will. I'm going to zip down toward Paisar and go around behind it. Maybe 45 minutes, we'll be in flatter water. Looks like you got your sea legs back, huh.

—A night's sleep on the ocean, usually does it.

CHAPTER 19

Bo, replete with breakfast, lifting binoculars as the Walter rounds the south end of Peisar Island. Two boats visible trolling northwest, one resolving itself through the lens as the Sobrino. Not sure about the other, might be that little double ender, the Hannah. About two miles off…I'll just run past this shallow ground and put the gear in. Time for a coffee refill...Jesus I hope they're still biting, feel so stupid running around with the gear out of the water on a one-day opening.

Remnant swells coming through the channel between Biorka Island and the Neckers beginning to roll the Walter as Bo turns to the northwest. Wind chop smacking the port side planks. Not exactly flat calm here. But it looks better ahead. There we go, bottom's dropping to 30 fathoms.

—C'mon Reilly let's get the gear back in.

All four lines deployed, Bo expectantly perched on edge of trolling hatch. Chop easing in the expansive lee of Biorka Island, the Walter trolling smoothly on to the northwest. Implacable silence from the pole tips. No fish biting, no bells ringing, internal storm clouds beginning to gather. What the fuck. Maybe the morning bite's over. Maybe Wade caught them all. God damn it I hate this chasing other people's fish trying to catch the ones they caught before you got there and half the time getting nothing. Fuck. And look out there, the horizon's all torn up just like it was coming out from Lazaria, I suppose we're going to get thrashed on this side too. That little boat's turning around. Can almost make out the name, yep it's the Hannah. Somebody in the trolling hatch, let's see what he's doing...pulling a fish. Looked like a nice one, too. Jesus Christ, there's another one on the next spread.

—Reilly, God damn it, where's our fish?

What's Wade up to. Just getting out into the slop out there, starting to rock around pretty good. There, he's turning around too, I'll edge out and give him some room, impolite to crowd a guy on his own spot.

Bell on port deep line jerking insistently.

—At last. Jesus! I guess they're all out here on this end of the tack. Maybe if we keep following this depth curve farther out, it'll pay off. Though it looks pretty rough out there. But we're used to it, right? You can handle it okay Reilly?

— I don't remember any of this macho fight-the-weather fishing last year.

—How about that time the wind came up sudden out on the Fairweather?

—We didn't have much choice then, six hours

from an anchorage. Now, we do.

—Look, it's safe. The Walter can no doubt take more than we can. We'll just go a half mile farther, this tack. I'm going to pull this fish now, make sure the hook doesn't get ripped out when we start rolling.

Bo engaging the gurdy. Waving across two hundred yards of rain-pocked water at the Sobrino passing by to port. Arguello waving back from his trolling hatch. Someone else on board there, his nephew? Although he looks smaller than I remember...aha, here's our fish. And there's the serious rollers just ahead. Come on, brother, let's get you aboard before it gets jerky.

Following the 35-fathom line's curve around Biorka, the Walter making a gradual turn to quarter into the rising seas, explosions of spray off the port bow. The boat reeling across the ocean's tortured surface in reprise of the morning's agonizing performance. Bo pushing on into the rough zone for twenty minutes before reversing course and, with commotion eased, running the three remaining lines for five kings. Settling into a routine, Bo alternating sides to run lines, Reilly dressing fish and sliding them forward to drop down into the hold. The three boats spread out along a mile and a half trolling back and forth. A polite little fleet, respectful of convention that the boat with beach to starboard takes right of way. Fish biting sparsely but predictably, six or seven per circuit, mostly climbing on at the outer end of the drag. Wind and seas continuing undiminished, late afternoon yielding an occasional tantalizing glimpse of blue through the low cloud sweeping to the east.

This thing's blowing itself out, by tomorrow there won't be much left. For what that's worth, which is not much since we can't fish past midnight. Here comes the Sobrino heading back, Wade's passing a little closer this time. Wave even though he's in the far side of the hatch. Deckhand on near side, leaning over a fish, giving a friendly wave, almost looks like...

—Holy shit it's Karen.

— Who's Karen?

—Oh, uh, someone I didn't expect to see with Wade.

So much for her concern that I not be getting it on with any of her friends. Want to yell, hey what's fair about this. Although since I'm the one called it off I suppose I don't have much say. But still seems kind of rash. On Wade's part too, the jerk. Though at least he's never been anything but up front, about how cool he thought she was...but still...

—Aren't you going to pull that fish Bo?

Bo grabbing the snap which has been jerking against the wire and hauling a hefty if fatigued Chinook up close. Sorry I didn't mean to ignore you, feel free to come aboard.

Three more tacks, catch rate slipping. Light leaking fast out of the sky. In deep dusk, Bo pulling the gear aboard and aiming back toward the east end of Peisar. The Sobrino there two miles ahead, red light appearing as Arguello makes the left turn toward Sitka.

—You getting me here Wade?

—He's in the fish hold Bo. You never told me fishing was this much fun.

—Oh yeah, fun if you like getting bashed around.

—It didn't seem all that bad. You were the one that kept going out in the rough zone. Oh, here's Wade. It was good to see you, Bo.

—Yeah, likewise, I guess. Well Wade, you get happy?

—Happy enough I guess, got 55 or so. How'd you do?

—A lot better than if I'd stayed on the other side, that's for sure. Thanks for that. I wonder how it went up at Salisbury.

—I talked to Gary about an hour ago, you forgot the sideband check in? It was poverty up there. Best score he heard was 12.

—Wow. Sucks for them. Guess that means the price will hold up for July, anyway.

—I'm sure they're all looking on it in that optimistic way. I'd better pay attention here, just coming out into the open and the hatch covers aren't on yet.

—See you at the dock then.

The Walter retracing path through the swell coming in through Necker Channel. Remnant evening light reflecting off occasional whitecaps through forward windows. Reilly climbing out of hold after icing the catch, shucking oilskins in cabin and coming forward to gaze pensively ahead.

—Well that didn't turn out so bad, did it. You get a count? What did we wind up with, around thirty?

—Thirty-two.

—Could be worse, huh. Considering we spent the morning in hell. How about salmon and broccoli, it'll be kind of rolly once we get away from Peisar but not too bad, you feel like cooking?

—If you want.

Bo peering over.

—What's going on Reilly? You've been, like, uncharacteristically subdued all afternoon.

—Bo, how about if we anchor up before going in?

—You mean the hot spring? I don't know Reilly, we've got to get these fish off and the hold cleaned before our ice appointment tomorrow, there's going to be a bunch of boats ahead of us on the unloading list—

—Just for a while, we don't have to stay.

—Well...I suppose we could. Can't take the inside passage through all those wash rocks in the dark, so it'd be a rough shitty run in. And from what Wade says, the rest of the fleet won't have much of anything to deliver. Okay, we'll take the chance. I guess it's been pretty rough, your first day back on the ocean. That what's bothering you?

Reilly continuing to stare forward, arms folded hugging herself.

—No. I didn't tell you, I had a long talk with Max just before we left yesterday. He says he wants to call it all off.

—What?

—I didn't take it seriously. But the more I think about it, he wasn't kidding. It's over, Bo.

—Aw, he can't mean it. After all this time you've been together?

—Yeah, he could, you don't know him.

—Still, I—oops, here we are. Can you take the lantern out and find this rock that's showing on the radar just ahead off to starboard? We'll drop the hook just the other side of it.

Reilly exiting jacketless, going forward to sweep the light until it picks out a dark hump looming up out of darker water, seaweed at the tide line glistening in the flashlight beam. Bo idling past to stop off a larger treed islet lying offshore the beach, grabbing jacket and joining Reilly on the bow.

—Go on in and get dry. I'll get this set.

The Forfjord dropped and scope let out, wind swinging the Walter around. Bo going in and backing to set the anchor. Switch off running lights, pull fuel cutoff lever and take in the sudden quiet of the engine's absence. Background sounds of the wind, wavelets lapping the hull planks. Reilly standing by the stove's warmth.

—So, you want to get towels and stuff, I'll start getting the skiff down?

—Oh Bo, I don't want to go through all that hassle, I just wanted to stop and think, I just—God Bo I feel so empty—

Crossing the cabin to lean head against Bo's shoulder, still hugging stomach tightly. Bo acceding to tug on heart, arms out and around in comforting embrace. Her arms circling his waist in response. That animal heat again, like in the truck the other night, Jesus I shouldn't get turned on here…

—Look Reilly, I still don't think anyone could change that radically that fast. I mean, it can take months and months to get over someone you've been close to. Hell, maybe it takes years…I'm sure he's reacting to the suddenness of you saying you wanted space—

—No. Max makes up his mind on something and then that's it. I know, I've lived with him for three years. The weird thing is, it's only now that the bridge might be burned it feels like I'll never find anything as nice as what I had, Bo, I still just feel so alone.

—Yeah, well that's natural but I'm sure you'd find someone easily, if it came to that, only I don't see how it would, Max'll maybe back off for a while but it's not in human nature to

—Bo—

—cut off our emotions like that, we pretend we can but they'll eventually work their way back to the surface, and then we just have to

—Bo, I—

—take stock of our situation, think reasonably about it, and begin to work toward a solution, maybe get some counseling, it's not like you're really alone, plenty of other couples have been down this road, there's probably a whole body of literature on—

—Bo!

Her arms tightening suddenly, Bo surprised by

their force looking down at her wet insistent face—
—Bo, will you—Bo, please just shut up and—

CHAPTER 20

Bo rising at first indication of light in cabin to pull anchor. Coming back in past settee, last night's scene recreating itself, surely there were many reasons why not but I could not resist the rising desire the smell of skin next to her sweater's wet wool her hungry lingual exchange as we fumbled out of clothes. Reilly backing up onto settee taking me in and wrapping legs around, moaning and pressing close arms tight around neck, the table corner jutting into ribs let me lift us down onto the floor. Intent to make love gently going nowhere, insistent hands on my back pulling me to more violent thrusts tears filling her eyes convulsing in shuddering climax and me left lying depleted and sad among discarded pants and boots.

Now taking the wheel and motoring out of the bay's still water. Jesus what have you got yourself into. Fishing can't handle much distraction and now we're totally disoriented. But maybe it was just momentary catharsis and we'll go on as before. I hope so.

Out past black whale shaped Naerie Rock and into a morning of broken clouds and gusty northwest wind, whitecaps ice bright in sunny patches. Foreboding displaced by need to concentrate in the tortuous rockridden channel past Povorotnoi Point. Open water beyond much smoother than on the trip out, swell down and only moderate wind chop. Reilly appearing, awkwardness during the making of coffee but a half smile delivered with hot mug. Taking Middle Channel south of Japonski Island and radioing in while passing under the Harbor bridge, lucking into a gap in the unloading list and tying up to the Southeast dock. Modest trip soon bucketed out of hold, Bo pitching ice while Reilly scrubs bin boards on deck, dropping into hold with brush and bucket as Bo climbs ladder for the weigh-up. Untying and heading for Thompson.

—Seems like we can still work pretty efficiently together, despite last night's, ahh, episode, ahh, that could have had the potential to be, well, disruptive? I mean, um, to the good working relationship we had last year?

—Very succinctly put, Bo.

—Come on, we have to talk about it don't we?

— I suppose. Okay, I'm not sure what was going on, but I don't think it has to change anything. I mean, for fishing? Don't you think?

— I just don't want things to get complicated.

—Well, you just keep on being Mr. Simple Straightforward guy, and I'll follow along. How's that?

—Sounds…doable. So, to start, I think I'll go straight forward to the Lincoln for breakfast after we tie up, you want to come?

—I think I'll go straight down to my bunk and catch up on the sleep I missed. How about the rest of the day?

—Groceries, then we get ice at three. Other than that, we're pretty much ready to leave late afternoon, get some good distance toward where we'll start on Friday. So you can be here ready to go around one?

—I'll be here.

Local Troller Picked for Board of Fish Slot

By Myra Wooley

Alaska Board of Fisheries Chairman Charlie Petersen announced Thursday that he has nominated Rick Corvis of Sitka to fill a vacant Board position. Corvis, who would be the first Sitkan on the Board since…well, forever…says that he is proud and more than ready to take on the complicated job of overseeing the State's fisheries.

"My nomination indicates the long overdue desire to bring a more practical approach to fisheries management, which is what I'm all about. Alaska Fish and Game is beginning to understand that getting data and insight from fishermen is just as important as being preoccupied with a lot of "scientific" (make sure you put that in quotes) studies which mostly they just show that somebody took a class in grant writing. Now we're going to think outside the bag. Why not try some new fisherman-inspired ideas? Like how about this: real time input. Every fisherman's got a sideband radio; with a little wireless mike and some software, we could have them report every fish right when they catch it! And if they catch the wrong kind of fish, we can invoke an immediate spot closure and make them move somewhere else. Total communication, 24/7, it takes all the guesswork out of managing! And maybe we could sell some of the incidental data to marketers, like what kind of sodas the fishermen are drinking? That would pump up the Department's budget. Plus I have some safety ideas, like mandating sprayed foam in enough interior spaces of every boat that it couldn't possibly sink. And another I'm working on, what if we had everyone tow their liferaft off the stern, fully inflated at all times, so it's always ready in case of fire or whatever."

Corvis had a lot more to say but it was way more than this article has space for.

The Board seat became open when Homer charter fisherman Tosh Underhatch announced he would be vacating the post soon after former Governor Jenna Impale left office early to take up a career as a motivational speaker and eyewear consultant. According to a Knowledgable Source who wished not to be identified, the two were "very close, wink wink".

Corvis' nomination must be approved by new Governor Ted Hermiston. Exactly when that might happen is unclear, but it will be "soon," said an impatient, irritable, not very polite spokesman reached at the Governor's number after repeated calls.

□

CHAPTER 21

Counter at the Lincoln. Bo waving the Watchdog as Arguello materializes next stool to the west.

—You see this? Gertie Rick's up for the Board of Fish! The salmon fishery's gonna be overseen by a totally loose cannon.

—Yeah, well at least he's our loose cannon. That last guy, trying to reallocate all the salmon to the charter sector. With his agenda, only way we could keep earning a living would be as party boat guides, baiting hooks for tourists. 'Excuse me, sir, would you prefer a herring, or a candlefish this morning? A herring, excellent choice, sir.'

—And, 'Oh dear, sir, I'll get a mop and clean up that vomitus right away, so sorry about these waves.' You've got a point.

—Early self-inflicted death clearly a more attractive option.

—But at least we always knew where Underhatch was coming from. With Rick, who knows. I just hope they don't give him free rein with all his crazy ideas. Speaking of free rein —

Setting paper aside and attempting stern glare at friend.

—You didn't waste much time moving in on Karen, did you.

Arguello returning gaze.

—It was pretty clear you'd moved out on her. You having second thoughts, now?

—Well no. But you might have at least observed a brief period of mourning.

—Rest assured. We mourned for a full hour at the Quixote. So, you done with your insupportable complaint, ready to be happy for me now I've found a crew might turn out to be as good as yours?

—Yeah, Reilly, that's a whole nother story…so Karen's going to work out? Wow, who knew she was interested in fishing.

—Anybody that might've had the intelligence to ask?

—Yeah well. So, what about Alsea?

—Go ahead and invite her if you like. But I think she'd rather go shopping.

—I didn't mean…okay, I guess I can't come up with any reason to hold a grudge. I'd offer to whup you at cribbage, but I'd better get moving if I'm going to make it out of port this afternoon. You gonna be ready?

—Yep, gear and groceries soon after I get my coffee here, then ice, then split. I talked to Gary, he's shooting for five o'clock, how's that with you.

—I'll be tuned in to the funny radio.

CHAPTER 22

Driving out Halibut Point Road to SeaMart and its greater grocery selection. Returning to deposit the multitude of plastic bags on the Walter to be stowed by Reilly. Then, with an hour still remaining before ice appointment, racing aimlessly around town in pickup trying to fight off anxiety about where to start the season. Winding up in the NAPA parking lot. Go on! Buy a wiper blade, It's crazy to keep driving around in the rain with half the windshield blurred. Yeah but without craziness life is just all oppressive and serious. It'll be plenty oppressive if you run into a tree in a downpour. I'm not gonna run into any tree.

Snapping out of paralysis and driving bladeless back to the boat. Reilly aboard pouring hot water into a mug, the cabin straightened up and ready. Leftover tension somewhat eased. Maybe we'll get back to normal after all.

—Want some tea?

—Sure, might calm me down a little. Let's see, what kind.

Leaning past Reilly to examine arrayed boxes above stove. Boat listing slightly as someone climbs aboard. Bo turning as Myra steps through the door.

—Hi Bo, I wanted to—

—Myra, hi, how did—

—I wanted to say goodbye, Julie told me where you tie up, I brought these plum blossoms they're…supposed to bring good luck...

Her eyes going between Reilly and Bo, standing close. Bo finally getting the presence of mind to move to center of cabin.

—Ahh thanks that's really nice, oh, this is my crew Reilly, um, that is, Cathleen, Cathleen Reilly. Oh, and this is Myra, Wooley…

Bo's tongue developing a strange paralysis. Myra looking around, taking in the folded quilt and pillows at back of settee, small glass with forget-me-nots Reilly has bungeed in the galley window. Aura of alarm.

—But…maybe you've already got all the luck you need? Maybe I—I'll see you Bo, have a good trip.

Laying flowers on table, turning to door, climbing back down to the dock. Bo breaking out of inertia, jumping down after, catching up.

—Myra wait, I—I'm glad you came—

—You just disappeared the other morning, I tried to believe it was something important…but now you're going to leave without saying goodbye. I guess I get it, it just didn't mean anything, did it.

—No, no, it wasn't, I just get distracted right before the season opener, I—

—Maybe I should thank you for taking a little time off from your domestic scene, to spend a night with me?

—It's not a domestic scene. She's my deckhand, crewed for me last summer, and then came back this season—

Do you sleep with her?

—No. Well, not exactly, we—

Oh shit how do I explain this. I'm fucked.

—What? 'Not exactly?' What's that mean? How naive do I seem? Oh Bo I thought you were a straight up man, now I don't—

Green eyes filling with pain, tears, turning away, receding up the dock.

—Myra—

Oh, shit.

CHAPTER 23

Bo in dark blue mood, casting off and motoring down channel to tie up to barnacled low-tide pilings, pulling on oilskins and insulated gloves and climbing into hold. Reilly helping from above to muscle the jerking hose around as Bo directs a frigid rush of ice chips into the bins. Icy mist filling the hold as Bo smoothes mounds and distributes foam blankets. Climbing back up to sign invoice that appears in a bucket lowered from the dock.

—Thanks Dave.

—Good luck.

Lines loosened and pulled aboard. On the slow motor up channel, Bo pulling out phone to text. How do I say this in 160 characters.

I don't want us to end. It's not what you think I swear. Will explain when I get back. Please give me a chance.

The harbor growing smaller astern for half an hour until the turn past Halibut Point Park and a few picnicers. Now, the dreary prospect of listening to the engine shove the boat along through the rest of this day and all of tomorrow, until the season legally begins the following morning. Bo putting on headphones, cuing up 'Rain King'. *Render up my body into the burning heart of God in the belly of a black-winged bird*, that's about right. Turn up the volume on these hard driving major chords.

Making it through Olga Strait and its giant kelp patch and past the rock in Neva the Cavalier ran hard aground on a few years ago, heading out for the king opener just like we are, that would take your mind off your emotional problems wouldn't it.

The channel widening at St. John the Baptist, easing the need to concentrate.

—Reilly. Let's get some more leaders tied up. You want to do the spoons, I'll take hootchies?

The pile of coiled leaders growing. Repetitive job displacing some pain. Past Klokachef Island and into an ocean barely ruffled by a northerly breeze. Bo pulling on dark glasses, forced by sun glare on water to acknowledge the unclouded sky of a beautiful evening.

—Looks better than last time we were out, anyway.

—True, hmm. Look, Bo—was that somebody you care about? Myra?

—Well...we've just started seeing each other, but...yes, I guess I have to say it is.

—So, wow, I didn't have any idea, I'm sorry if I screwed things up with you but—why didn't you say something? Out at the hot springs?

—You wanted me to just shut up, remember?

—Well, that shouldn't...okay I don't suppose

analyzing it helps. But, if there's anything I can do…

—How about, you'll testify you took advantage of me?

—Well...is that the kind of expert courtroom testimony you get five hundred an hour for?

—Depends on how expert you are, at taking advantage of innocent unsuspecting men.

—Ha ha. I said I'd help, but I'm not committing perjury.

Bo laying course on plotter to pass inside Olga Rock. Weird, the urge to get close enough to this underwater hazard to see it. Like circling around something embedded in your subconscious, something you know you need to work on, if you could only get a good look at it. But on this smooth ocean, Olga won't have its breaker, best to stay a safe distance off. Could listen to the forecast now but why bother, the weather's gonna be what it is.

Just like me, maybe. Predestined, to just be a fuckup with women. Except you'd think a human would be more capable of independent action than a bunch of pressure gradients. Unless you're an animist, believing that even clouds have souls. But would a cloud think 'Oops, I dumped a bunch of rain on that picnic, I'm so sorry'? Doesn't seem likely. Even animals…

—Do you know dogs pretty well Reilly?

—What? Sure, why?

—Have you ever seen a dog act like it wanted to take back something it did?

—No, not really. But if a dog thinks you're angry

with it, it might *look* regretful. Which is probably learned behavior, because it knows then you'll feel sorry for it and stop being angry. What dogs do, and us too to a degree, is what we've been rewarded for doing, and we avoid what we've been punished for. At least, that's what behaviorists say.

—So, would a behaviorist say we can modify our own behavior? Reward and punish ourselves for our actions?

—I don't know about behaviorists. But Kant figured that humans are the only ones that can act out of reason, rather than instinct, the way animals have to. So the dog, at least, is off the hook, you see what I'm saying?

—Yeah…maybe…

—He also said that the *intent* to act with good will is the only real good. Even though we can conceive of a kind of universal morality, it doesn't really mean anything unless we act on it. If we don't, the selfishness will pile up and wreck everything. And even though we might be smart, or brave, or whatever, it doesn't mean much unless we will ourselves to act morally.

Bo scratching his head.

—So, just good intentions are enough to—

—On the other hand, you have Spinoza saying that there's no such thing as free will, that our thoughts result from a chain of cause and effect, as willed by God, and—

—Wait, who now?

—Spinoza, you know, Dutch, seventeenth

century? You'd think that attributing everything to God would've been pretty popular back then, but he went on and said that even God didn't have a choice about how He made the world, and worse heresy, he said God didn't care what happened to us. That got him kicked out of the Jewish religion, and it didn't gain him any traction with Christians either—

—What's that have to do with—

—anyway, what Kant concluded was that you might be a naturally good person, but if you act morally without thinking about it, it's not worth much compared to someone who has the *intent* to act in the name of good. Even if they don't succeed. Maybe it would help if I explained his idea of the categorical imperative, compared to the hypothetical, you want me to?

—No! I mean, maybe some other time, Reilly. Jesus, there's been a lot of philosophy around lately. I wonder if it's another side effect of global warming…I gotta check in with those other guys.

Pulling down the CB microphone.

—You get me here Gary? Pick me up Wade?

—Hey Bo what's up?

— Charging along on a beautiful ocean, trying not to get hung up on catheter imperatives…you out here?

—What was that? We're just coming up on Khaz Bay. I thought that might've been you back there. How far you going?

—My plan's to run tonight, get out to the Fairweather Grounds in time to look around some tomorrow.

—Same here. Gary, too. We'll see you out there.

Bo paralleling the rocky Chichagof shore, watching the sounder. A few boats nosing around closer in, likely specialists who adopt a spot and stay there all season. A comfortable approach, get to know all the local fish-aggregating pinnacles, drive the same route every day, sleep every night in a familiar anchorage. Take what shows up instead of charging madly around looking for the big scores. But what if the fish don't show up and you catch nothing, how do you keep from going crazy? Better stick to charging around madly.

The north-skewed solsticean sun doing a slowmotion dive past the horizon. Burning orange through a thin verge of far distant clouds. Light ebbing slowly from the sky. Bo switching on nav lights, noting with satisfaction the white gleams of two sternlights a couple of miles ahead.

Past the White Sisters, Bo changing course to angle directly out toward the Fairweather Bank. Resisting a pull in toward Cape Cross, where the Yakobi Island shore bends in toward Cross Sound. Along which massive tidal ebbs and flows stir up feed and create perfect conditions for hungry salmon to dally. Notorious trolling drags along there, Surge Bay, the Podium, Hoktaheen. At each of which, in a day and a half, there'll be a big tight fleet of boats going around and around in a circle, taking turns to pass the sweet spot where the fish school up. Have to be constantly vigilant, stay just close enough to the boat ahead to keep certain greedy fuckers from cutting in line, and far enough back to give the fish a chance to regroup before your lures wiggle enticingly past. Huge first-day scores possible there if you don't mind getting dizzy and angry at the same time.

Bo gauging distance on plotter. Seven hours to the edge of the Bank, it'll be five in the morning before we can start looking around. Better figure out a watch schedule.

—Reilly, how about if I go till one o'clock, you take it the next four hours?

—Sounds fine to me. Guess I'll turn in, then.

Bo settling into pilot seat with mug of cocoa. Turning down sounder and plotter intensity in the now-dark cabin. Muted glows punctuated by occasional red and green blinks from the Comnav control as the autopilot kicks the rudder port and starboard. Hypnotic hum of engine, Walter rolling gently in low swell. Could almost relax here, stress of all that preseason work and emotional discord fading as the distance from Sitka grows. Some jazz would be nice...Brubeck, yes, this warm cabin and the Brandenburg Gate might get me close to nirvana.

Time passing easily until one a.m. and Bo hollering down into focsle. Reilly emerging and filling the cabin with coffee aroma as Bo flips the table leaf and snuggles into covers on the settee and contented sleep. Reawakened some hours later by the VHF.

—What was that? What time is it?

—Quarter to five, it was the Coast Guard. I think

they might have been calling us.

—What? Shit, what could that be about.

Bo rising, turning the volume knob and testing squelch.

—Walter K. Coast Guard Juneau Com Center calling the Walter K.

—Coast Guard Juneau, this is the Walter K.

—Walter K, can you switch and answer channel 22 alpha.

—Roger, switching.

—Good morning skipper. Do you have a Cathleen Reilly on board there.

—Roger, she is aboard.

—We have an urgent request for her to call her brother at the following number, regarding a family emergency. 707 883 2857. How do you copy.

—I copy that. Is that all the information you have?

—Roger skipper.

—Thank you...Walter K clear, back to 16.

—Oh my God—what could it—how do we call?

—I'm sure there's no cell coverage here. Closest would be Elfin Cove...hold on, Gary's got a satellite phone, let me....

—You picking me up here Gary?

—Yeah Bo, I heard that exchange with the Coast Guard, I'm sorry.

—Yeah. Could you make a sat phone call to that

number for us?

—*Sure. Give it to me again.*

Bo slowing the engine down to idle. Long minutes passing until Gary's voice returns.

—*Okay, here it is. I talked to your brother, Reilly. Your parents were in a pretty bad auto accident, they're in the hospital in Santa Rosa, Mike thinks you should come.*

Bo handing the microphone over.

—Anything else, did he say anything else?

—*Yeah ...they're both in critical condition. That was all he had...sorry, Reilly.*

Bo revving the engine and wheeling around to a northeasterly course, engaging the autopilot and turning to offer a consoling embrace. Imagining broken bodies on a highway. Our lives fracture so suddenly. Amazing we don't spend all our time wondering where the next hit is coming from.

—Okay, we have to figure out how to get you down there. We'll head for the Cove, get a float plane to take you to Juneau, you can fly to California from there. We're about seven hours away. I'll ask Gary to make another call around eight when the float plane office opens, see if they'll send a plane out.

Sun rising from behind the Fairweather Range. Golden rays ricocheting off the magnificent high snow covered peaks usually hidden in clouds, now through tense ambiance in cabin seeming only stark and cold. Time and miles passing with excruciating slowness. Occasional small specks ahead growing to reveal themselves as other trollers heading out. Which, hopefully, I will be doing before this day is gone. And possibly without crew, on this most important week of the whole summer. Unless I luck out and can find someone on the docks in there.

Bars on Bo's cell phone an hour out, confirming arrangements to bring a plane. Reilly taking phone out onto the foredeck, punching keys and starting a long conversation full of gestures before re-entering.

—That was weird, Max was almost as freaked out as I am. He's going to pick me up at the airport…I guess we're not over after all.

—Huh. Well…that's great.

Lifting the poles and navigating through rocks outside the Cove's entrance and finding an empty slip along the dock. Reilly heading for seaplane float with minimal baggage, Bo escorting. A final, filial hug. Rotors accelerating, the plane taxiing out of the harbor and with huge assault of noise lifting and banking sharply to disappear to the east.

That's that then.

Bo taking the waterfront boardwalk that circles the small hill on which the village clusters, checking fish buyer's office, café, various bulletin boards finding no leads. One last try in the sportfishing lodge, yeah there were a couple guys were staying here looking for work, gave up and left this morning to camp in the forest service cabin at White Sulphur, don't know how you'd contact them other than going down there.

Likely a ten hour fool's errand, forget that. Crewless for the king opener, what a disaster. But okay, this is what we've got. Go back to the boat and get the hell out of here.

Out into open water again and a thin steady stream of boats coming out into Cross Sound from Juneau and Hoonah and the other inside ports, most heading down toward the Yakobi shore, a few angling out toward the Fairweather grounds. My scouting opportunity is shot. It'll take me all day just to get back out there, and if I want to start on the West Bank I'll be running most of the night too. Could take the easier option, slip on down to Surge Bay and anchor for the night, start out there in the morning all rested up. But there's no way to fight those crowds and stay on the drag unless someone's driving at all times and when I'm down in the fish hold icing I'm blind. Stick with the original plan. At least it's a nice ocean for running.

This optimistic view proving unsustainable as several hours out the breeze organizes itself into a rising northwesterly. By the time the Walter has cleared the coast enough that the still clear Fairweather Range reappears, the bow is smashing into sharp five-foot wind waves, spray blowing back. Good we got that rainex on, water's sliding right off the windows and I've got a clear view of those mountains but we are down to five knots now and I still can't appreciate the scenery. Fuck a duck, this trip just keeps sliding downhill.

Memory jogged to a totally flummoxed Wade in

Yakutat an August past, well into a bottle of single malt with bent hydraulic steering ram half dismantled on the dock, taking a mighty but ineffectual pound on it with a five pound maul before shaking his fist at the sky and yelling

—Come down here and fight like a man you mean-spirited son of a bitch!

The blasphemy eliciting no stroke of lightning from above but no answer to his mechanical puzzle either. The universe does not care about us at all is the most positive take from that scene. If I continue in this desolate line of thought I can see myself retreating to Elfin Cove. Spend the king opener drinking in the Coho Bar. To avoid this option I will investigate whether a good meal might help the mood.

Bo lurking in the door, timing dash to fish hold in between bursts of spray and retrieving ribeye and zucchini. This being the last meal when I'll have plenty of time to cook, might as well make it a good one, boil water for rice and dice garlic and ginger to simmer this steak in. Look on the bright side, with no crew to consume half the food I'll be able to go twice as long. Which I'll probably have to, if I want to get any kind of a load on board doing all the work myself. Oops that borders on irony, close neighbor to despondency. Immerse nose in tantalizing aroma.

Distraction lasting through dish cleanup, subsequent return to watching plotter and fighting self pity. Evening radio check revealing partners on west bank, Antigone on the outside edge, Sobrino farther along to the northwest, having found little feed to enthuse about along the way. Bo predicting late arrival on east bank, signaling intent to try there in the morning rather than run through the night and into exhaustion. Three hours more of crashing through the dark, shutting down after midnight to drift near the 13-fathom high spot. Out on deck to deploy stabilizers and look around. Several dozen scattered mast lights, most a few miles north around Fleet Corner. The Walter, stern quarter to the seas, riding comfortably enough. This weather no fun for traveling but should be okay for fishing.

Alarm sounding at four, Bo jumping into routine with hope-filled energy. Can't get along on three hours sleep the whole trip, but better hit it hard the first day. Coffee and the weather report, little change next few days, that's okay then. Engine's warm, I'm awake, let's get the gear in. Start with an easterly pass inside the 13, extend it for a ways, hearing no big jangle of bells, turn around for a back tack. Run through six lines for four average sized kings. Not the pace we're looking for. The other boats consolidating on the corner. Better go join the crowd. Half an hour away, can mute the growing nervousness by cleaning and icing this handful of fish.

Fitting into the fleet, tacking back and forth over a steep underwater slope that rises from 50 to 30 fathoms, a spot famous for big scores. But fame not in the cards this day. Running the gear after an hour and landing six kings. Another hour for five. And three, the next. Mid-morning radio check coming up, hope for salvation, it has to be better where those guys are and in two hours I could be there too.

News from the west bank however offering no encouragement. Wade accompanying his report of 18 fish with a tirade against the gods of luck, Gary with 21 and a rumor heard on another channel about good scores on the inner bank.

Bo considering this as he goes through five lines for two kings. And notes that there are fewer boats than when he arrived. Scanning to the northeast, sees two vees getting smaller. This place was not all that healthy to begin with and is now dying. Three hours run to the inside bank. The slow part of the day coming up, wouldn't sacrifice too much fishing time—let's do it. Leave this lead in the holder, get in the bow line this side and then the float. And please, God of Luck, it was Arguello who disrespected you and not me, so don't put four surprise fish on my last line and make me crazy with doubt about this move.

Said God happy enough to comply by putting no fish on any remaining line. Bo setting course for the raised stretch of bottom north and west of Lituya Bay. Once clear of the little fleet, cleaning the last few salmon and following them down into the hold to pack into ice. Twenty fish, a lousy start but better than nothing and hope still alive. Guess I was wrong last night, got plenty of time to cook again, which is good since breakfast forgot to happen. Oh man I hope this move works out.

One omelet and two anxiety-ridden hours later,

Bo sighting the first poles of a fleet which resolves itself as he nears into a group of forty or so boats tacking over a finger-like underwater peninsula that extends east from the bank. Boats pretty spread out, meaning, one hopes, there's a fair sized body of fish. Get the gear in out here and ease into this gap between boats, like merging on the highway. There's a bell already. And another. Maybe I get to make something of this day after all.

Bo angling in and out through the boats when possible, trying to get a feel for the feed pattern below and its attending fish school. Bells sounding with slow but steady frequency, the gear yielding six or seven fish each time through. Can't complain, not the rush we had in Salisbury but plenty to keep busy with.

The pace continuing through late afternoon then dropping off. The fleet concentrating on the east end of the finger. Damn, now it's going to get competitive, not enough fish here for this many boats. Everybody closing in, making shorter tacks. Have to keep peering around the cabin to see who's coming the other way. Nothing fatal about colliding at two knots but nothing good about it either. Even if it's only the poles that sideswipe, the gear gets snarled and usually a pole breaks, you have to go in for repairs and lose the rest of the trip.

There's someone ahead, coming right down our course. Jog to the right a little, hope he's alert and considerate enough to turn a little so we pass easily. But he's not turning. Oh shit, it's the Breeze. Asshole

Mack who assumes the right of way is his because his big converted seiner's so intimidating. Well fuck you, I'm not moving any further.

Dark hull with broadly spread poles looming up. Bo's course taking the Walter clear, but her port float trailing directly in the Breeze's path. Boats coming abreast. One figure standing at the hatch cleaning, one lowering fish into hold—that's that jerk from the Quixote. And Mac in trolling pit running gear. All three oblivious, ostensibly, to Bo's presence a few dozen feet away. The Walter's float passing thirty feet in front of the Breeze's port bow wire. And on past the tip line. Bo holding breath anticipating the two lines fouling thirty fathoms down. Which somehow doesn't happen. Something wrong about this, he's the asshole and I'm the one all knotted up inside. Okay forget about it. Getting dark here and no fish biting, long as I'm aimed this way I might as well troll out and get clear of the fleet, go down and ice the fish that've been piling up. Then get some dinner started before pulling the gear in for the night.

Bo emerging from hold after forty minutes shoveling and icing. Sitting on hatch to cool off. Three quarter moon above, muted in remnant twilight. Wind's coming down. Should be good sleeping tonight. Oh boy.

Three hours later in max darkness, the ascendant moon illuminating the Fairweather Range in chill stark beauty. Mast lights of the sleeping fleet a small municipality drifting slowly in unison with the north-setting current.

CHAPTER 24

Clouds appearing southwest as Bo deploys gear in dim visibility well before sunup. Aiming toward last night's spot in scant hope the salmon have filled back in. But more likely after the way the fleet hammered this place, the fish are either all iced down, or moved on.

Bo making two passes for four kings. The scattered fleet concentrating again on tip of finger. Trying to catch yesterday's fish. The easiest approach, just keep grinding away here, try to believe they'll come on the bite again later…strong odds that won't happen. Fuck it.

Reaching the northwest end of the fleet, the Walter continuing on as other boats turn back. Their masts receding astern. Eyes on sounder, ears alert for bells, Bo fighting anxiety as time passes with no bites. Totally dead. This could be a desert that extends all the way to Yakutat. I could be exchanging a small sure thing for nothing at all. But can't give up and turn back, not yet. Pick up the gear and run? But where to? Better keep working this edge up to base of finger, hope either something's there or Wade and Gary have a good report.

Bo hanging up the microphone an hour later on ambiguous news. Partners, still exploring out on the west bank, reporting some modest success though looking to add up well under Bo's score from the day before. Not good enough to run to, at least not yet. Damn it. Keep trying this way for a while longer, hope this sinking feeling doesn't permanently knot up my gut.

An hour later where the 50-fathom line curves in to the east, as Bo finishes listlessly lowering yet another fishless line, the starboard bow pole jerking. And then the deep line. Joined by the starboard deep. Bo dashing into cabin to put mark on plotter. Oh yes, let this be it, let it be salmon and not some errant clutch of playful halibut.

A newly energized Bo running through the gear for nine fat salmon, turning around as bells go silent. Wielding cleaning knife, jumping up when bites resume to place new mark on plotter. So as to get a mental schematic of the school below. Not a huge school, but it looks like if I tack east and west staying just below this 42-fathom spot, I'll be—

—Oh shit.

Heretofore unnoticed intruders half a mile astern, spread out in formation side to side, their gear cooperatively sweeping a broad swath. Only one fleet operates like that, god damn, it has to be—the Breeze. And the Pastor, and the Michele Marie. I'm fucked. No way I can lead them off the spot, they're aimed right at me and it. And now, no way I can turn and make a back tack over it. Have to swing wide here, turn and pass through behind them north to south and hope—there's a bell—and another one. Must have just nicked the spot. And they must have hit it dead on, they're turning around now to go back through and I'm out of position again. Assholes appropriating my discovery. A sudden homicidal urge, repressed. Two ways to deal with this. Stay here and lock horns, try to dart in on this small bunch of fish when I can, get more and more pissed off. Or give up and look for another spot. And feel like a wimp.

What a choice. Fuck them, I'm not scaring off that easy.

Bo making a quick turn, setting up to return to original tack. Other three boats also turning, coming back opposite direction on a slow-motion collision course. Okay, they want to put it all on the line, I'm in. Aiming between Breeze and Michele Marie. Here we go then, they can spread out and let me through, or keep formation and tangle up. Which no sane person would do, everyone gets some damage…though maybe sanity doesn't enter into it, they don't seem to be moving—no, there, the Michele's turning slightly, just enough. Five feet between our poles. And now I have to look at all these fish being cleaned on their back decks. And asshole Mack lifting a big king aboard.

They hit the spot, all right. Which according to the plotter, I'm over right now. With no bells. No, there's one. And waiting for more...and waiting...fuck. That was no big pile of fish but it could've supported me for the rest of the day, now these rapists pass over it two or three times and it's as good as gone. I proved I'm not a pushover and so what. All right, time to move on, get out of this corrosive opportunistic meanspirited company. Go in and consider the plotter. That forty-fathom rise a few miles to the west, good a bet as any. Turn to 270 degrees and set pilot, get back in hatch and these few fish on deck. Slicing out the gills first. With occasional glances back at interloping fleet continuing back and forth. Who said it was okay for fuckheads like that to be on the planet. Wonder where they'd be on judgment day. With the establishment types who hang around by God, or the more honest fools getting thrown over the cliff?

Neither. They'd be God's gleeful devils slicing and skewering.

Noting jerk on port deep line but taking little pleasure. Let him drag for a while and keep cleaning. No, let's get him aboard, start the line up while I finish scraping this belly. Give an occasional push on the wire to keep it from piling up lopsided on the drum. Distracted by ongoing dark thoughts. Small steep sea hitting the hull, the deck lurching, Bo losing balance. Instinctively seeking stability, hand grabbing the wire. Cleaning knife dropped and preceding Bo's hand as the inspooling wire pulls both down into the winch drum. The knife jamming against mounting bolts and halting drum, keeping Bo's hand from being mangled but leaving it tightly clamped. Arm twisting weirdly, Bo reflexively resisting dislocation. Ending bent sharply at waist. Gasped oaths cut short as pain overload shuts down consciousness.

Waking after an indeterminate time to a world of pain and confusion. Holy fuck, what—what—screwing eyes against a tide of misery that slowly, slowly recedes, pain receptors weakening and growing numb. Awareness of different pain from back torqued in awkward position. Maybe if I lift my right leg up onto the hatch coaming. There that's better. Holy shit how do I get myself out of this. Can't reach the control valve, shoulder won't torque that far. Same with the clutch handle on the drum. Same with the autopilot control.

I'm helpless.

Oh this is fucked up.

Trying several more pulls, varying direction. No result other than more pain. Face it. I'm stuck.

Bo seeking what comfort is available, turning head and resting on edge of 3 X 10 hatch frame. Oh man. Calm down here and consider. This course taking me out into the middle of the Gulf, into nowhere. How about Wade and Gary, they'll notice when I don't come on the radio at check in. But they'll just think I'm busy. Maybe after a day or two, they'll worry? Or assume I just went back into port to get Reilly or something. Probably they won't think anything's wrong until they get in after this trip. A week from now, they might call the Coast Guard.

Might.

What else. Eventually we run out of fuel. The engine dies and the hydraulics stop and the line slacks and I get my hand back. How long till that happens. Let's see. Running on port tank which was full when we left Sitka. On the 29th. So seven hours that day, plus 24 the next, when Reilly got off, plus 24 more yesterday equals—but have to subtract some for sleeping—where was I fuck it's hard to think. Okay, start again. Seven, plus 24 minus four, twenty-seven. Plus another 20 for yesterday, 47. Plus today, it's about one now, equals—shit, where was I—okay 47 plus maybe eight…fifty-five hours…average one and a half gallons per hour…ah call it 60 hours make it easy… 90 gallons…tank holds 350…minus 90 is 260…at trolling speed only using one gallon per hour…so 260 hours…divided by 24…eleven days.

My God, can I last that long? People fast way longer, so wouldn't die of hunger. Thirst, though. Eleven days a very long time without water. Kidneys shriveling, blood cells dessicated like spawned out salmon in dried up arterial streams. Your tongue swells up, I've read. Wonder why that happens seems like it would shrink. It'll rain some time. Maybe I could reach my tongue down to the deck, lick up runoff. See if I can, ow! Maybe if I get desperate…what else on the killing list. Hypothermia. Warm here in this afternoon sun, with wool jacket and raincoat still on after icing. But if it continues clear tonight the heat'll get sucked out of here and if the wind picks up from east or north it'll carry the cold down off all that snow. Wonder if I could exercise somehow, keep my blood flowing around. Or would it weaken me more. Using energy just to hold this position, keep from slipping into the hatch and dangling from my arm.

That conch Gary got on his Bahamas trip, wanted to save the shell, to get the snail out he put a hook in its foot and hung it up overnight, its muscle gave up trying to support the weight of its own shell, stretched out two feet, Gary cut it off and had his trophy. But nobody around to cut me off. That climber got his arm stuck down in a canyon, knifed through it himself, they made a movie about it. Wonder if I've got the guts to do that. Moot point, no knife in reach except the one that's jammed below my hand, can just feel the spoon with my fingers. That's a good thing, isn't it, would think my hand would be totally numb by now, on the way to gangrene. Still wearing heavy insulated icing glove, jacket cuff caught in there too, just enough padding. Maybe not so good though, if the wire chafed all the way through my wrist I'd be free…but Jesus that's an awful image….

Bo zoning out.

Hard wood under cheek and temple. Engine vibration.

Steady low drone from exhaust stack.

Occasional slap of waves on starboard hull.

Eyes gradually focusing again on the shore receding astern. Upper part of La Perouse glacier coming into view. Above an ice face first seen ten years ago as dramatic bluewhite wall dropping directly into the sea, now shrunk to a dirty graveled slope back from the beach. Yet above, the same frozen river imperceptibly crawling toward the Gulf.

Bo shifting to new facial position. Thankful for absence of sharp edge or splinters on this board, worn smooth by my butt perched here countless hours waiting for jerk of line or bouncing float's signal a fish has latched on. All the salmon I've pulled over these boards. Maybe won't be any more.

The frozen river flashing Bo back in time and space to a muscular watercourse cutting the forest into a small anchorage partway up the inside passage. Encountered one autumn on trip south to boatyard in Port Townsend. A quick row ashore to stretch legs leading to several hours seated enthralled on mossy bank, where the stream gathers momentum and drops twenty feet to the bay below. The glassy perfection continuing smoothly over the edge like liquid poured out of a pail. Bo mesmerized by the point where the water just begins to accelerate. That point of no return. Which I would want to always inhabit, if it could be separated from the inevitable destruction below. Free of second-guessing, inevitably immersed in that smooth sinuous arc...a perfect form, like the top of an orange sun breaking the horizon...a beach breaker forming up to surfable shape...the sensuous curve of a woman's hip....

CHAPTER 25

—OK Bo you get me here?

Gary's voice, the CB speaker. Ow fuck why can't I move my arm…oh yeah right.

—Bo, you pick me up?

Wade coming back.

—Guess he's occupied. Couldn't get him on the sideband either.

—If I was a cynic I'd suggest he's up to his ass in salmon and can't be bothered to tell us…but I'd never suggest that. Would you?

—No, no, not our Bo. It is kinda weird though.

—Well. He mighta got hung up with something during the sideband check time, and he's probably out of range on this one.

—Yeah, I suppose. Well I hope he's catching more than I am. I'm starving here! Even though we just finished dinner.

—Might try working this way. I extended my tack off the edge. About three miles out here and had a pretty good pull last time. A few bells here now, too. What'd you have to eat? Small king on this boat.

—We grilled up a ling cod that came aboard this morning. Good and tender...yeah, I saw you out there and was wondering. Thanks on that Wade, I'll move on out.

Bo listening fascinated, appalled. At the homeliness of this exchange. Comparing meals and fishing just like always, oblivious of the fact I'm on a one way tack to slow death. I bet Karen did something real nice with that salmon. The cozy arrangement over there with Wade. Shit. I could get to feeling pretty sorry for myself—wait—they're working off the edge—that's going to put them pretty close to my course—damn! Let's see, I turned out around one yesterday, it's about 30 miles from the finger to the corner, at two knots about 15 hours, maybe add an hour cause I was further up on the bank, fuck man I could be trolling right through there early morning, right when they're putting the gear in, all alert—wind's come down, the ocean's almost glassy, they'll have to see me! Maybe this'll have a happy ending!

White hull creeping slowly west over an immensity of blue. Orange sun falling toward the horizon, the west face of the Fairweather Range turning pink. Then the wash of deep purple rising toward the high peaks. The long, cool darkening twilight. A few stars hazily appearing before the moon emerges and claims the night sky. Bo arranging himself as comfortable as possible, drifting hopefully to sleep with the boat's gentle rocking.

CHAPTER 26

After the long approach down Lisianski Inlet, the docks in Pelican at last. Plenty of empty slips, pick one here on the outside, easy to tie up with one hand. Someone up on the boardwalk waving—at me? No one else around down here…tossing a midships line onto the dock, stepping down to cleat off. The someone running down the ramp. A woman, severely cut short hair…

Bo's heart leaping and diving at the same time.

Mariella.

Rushing up and grabbing him in a fierce hug. Her torrent of explanation. The impossibility of forgetting him. End of school year, prospect of a free summer, going nowhere with Giovanni, the counsel of all her friends to follow her heart. Finally deciding to do it, chop her hair off and try something entirely new. Not knowing exactly where to find him but taking a chance and flying to Sitka. Asking in every marina there, at last directed to Julie and learning of the accident. The float plane to Pelican and here she was, was he glad to see her?

Glad, hurt, words insufficient. Bo struggling to adjust. Okay, well let's get your stuff onboard. Gravitating inexorably down into the focsle bunk. Armor built over seven months crumbling as they begin to make love, and Bo fighting tears all the way through to a deep, devastating release. His pain alchemizing, with the familiar smell, taste, touch of her, into the old deep intoxication.

Bo rationalizing a diversion to White Sulphur's hot spring to give his hand a chance to recuperate. And let Mariella get familiar with the boat before going back to fishing. A magical two days, then the return to Pelican to provision and gear up for an easy first trip, plan made to stay close to shore and anchorages. Finally, out the Inlet and passing the jagged rocks off Cape Spencer, heading west. Putting the gear in off Icy Point, Bo patiently explaining how to let the line out slowly enough to get the spoons and flashers snapped on. And then, as the first fish come aboard, how to dress and ice them.

Mariella's learning curve painfully slow, and as the first day wears on, flickers of doubt reinforcing a small dissident voice Bo tries to keep tamped down. Reminding himself, it's totally new to her, no reason to expect she'd get into it easily.

Anchoring for the night close to the beach in low seas, the next morning continuing the tack to the west, past the Glacier and on toward Lituya. Off the mouth of the Bay, finding a decent school. Mariella's speed at fish handling not improving, fish piling up in the checkers. Bo doing most of the cleaning, all the icing. Backlogged, catch rate plateauing. Injured hand again beginning to throb. The skeptic voice becoming assertive. Until after dinner on that second day. Mariella climbing down into trolling hatch, deliberately cleaning one fish with excruciating slowness, then turning.

—This isn't how I thought it would be. It is crazy to work this hard. We should take a break, Bo, show me this Lituya Bay you always talked about.

Bo trying to be patient, explaining this crucial part of the king season, that in order to have time off the rest of the year, they had to work the long hours, every day while it's open. That, sure, the work was hard, but it would certainly get easier after she got used to it.

—I will never get used to it. It is simple drudgery. You may keep on if you like. I will do the cooking but I will not clean any more fish.

Climbing out of the hatch and disappearing into the cabin. Bo left standing there. Only three days and I am reduced to the same pitiful fool. Ready to let my summer turn into a fruitless failure. Filling with a blind red anger, raising the gaff and smashing it violently on the rail.

CHAPTER 27

A small sharp sea smacks the Walter's port side, residual spray drifting down into the trolling hatch. Bo slowly surfacing—Christ—what a dream! So vivid, I thought—

Gradual recognition of a changed ocean. Blowing fifteen knots or so, easterly, looks like. Pretty light out, even with this cloud cover, must be well into morning—those guys, haven't seen me yet? Visibility's not that bad, we should be pretty close, I could try yelling. Yeah, that'd be stupid. Come on Bo try to be patient.

Like I have a choice.

The boat rocking on to the west. Bo shivering in the damp that's collected overnight. Steady hum of engine broken now and then by a wind gust. And at length by Wade's voice on the deck speaker.

—Get me here this morning Bo…Come on Bo, wake up and talk to me….

A pause, then Gary's reply.

—Guess he's not gonna.

—Guess not. Where are you?

—Just getting back into position. Got up before dawn to motor back east against this wind, nodded off and overshot it by a couple miles so I've been trolling back. How about you?

—I must have got into some weird current last night, I shut down a little to the inside and wound up almost where I'd started, even with the wind. Looks like the fish are still around.

—Yeah, I've been getting some bells all this way. Guess it's time to go rescue them. Okay Wade, I'll check you a bit later.

—Good going there Gary.

Fuck. What happened. Should've been right on their drag about now. I guess this wind pushed me away from them. God damn it! That was my big chance. My only chance...all right let's not freak out quite yet, maybe I was off on the figuring. Let's see, it was thirty hours at two knots, I think, that's fifteen hours, from...when was it from? When I started trolling out, or when I started calculating, was it one when I—or—fifteen, plus one is, sixteen, so—or—shit, I can't—well fuck it I don't even know what time it is now. Just hope I was a little slow, and only now coming into the area.

How it'll happen: they'll see me, they'll radio, I won't answer. They'll keep watching as I troll on west, making this totally goofy tack toward where there's never any fish, they'll have to think something's wrong, try calling again, then one of them will pull his gear aboard and chase me down.

Let's see they'll have to launch a skiff to come over and get me loose, kinda rough for that but Gary's got a good inflatable it'll be fine. Damn I hope this happens, soon, really getting thirsty now, mouth dry. Cold.

The day wearing on, gray and unchanging. A slight darkness above the eastern horizon astern the only sign of the Fairweathers, higher slopes obscured by cloud, foothills sunk below the earth's curve. A blackfoot albatross appearing, making a few gliding passes over the Walter's wake before fading off out of view. He didn't stick around long. No hope of morsels coming off this boat. No hope of anything. I missed them, they didn't see me. Or maybe they did. Didn't give a shit, maybe—the bastards. Caring for nothing but grubbing as many fish out of the ocean as they can. Gary with his big expensive plastic boat, gone totally straight with all the zeal he'd once had for his alternative save-the-planet outlook. And goddamn Wade, probably taking a mid day bunk break with Karen, the skinny satyrical fucker, her soft willing body yielding to—Jesus Bo shut the fuck *up*, if they knew they'd be here in a heartbeat what's the matter with you. Yeah, what's the matter. Not much other than being trapped like a fox in a leg clamp. Slowly dehydrating. Exhausted and cold yet starting to feel feverish, that's curious. What's curious about it. Who gives a fuck. Nothing you can do about it now, you're fucked. Oh yeah? Snivel and give up? Has to be a way out. Some way to get at the valve. Shoulder is what really prevents me from reaching anything. I could get my knees up onto the hatch coaming and somersault forward. My weight would break enough tendons and muscles, I could contort and reach the lever with my left arm? Jesus that's a sickening idea. But would it work. Try to climb up here and contemplate it. Ow fuck I…yeah, I guess I could maybe just get high enough to…but I can't see it. Can't see getting the flexibility I'd need, but a sure thing I'd tear my arm apart. Massive internal bleeding, die in intense pain instead of—what, there's something desirable about this low level pain? No come on, there's no better or worse, it's all just—I don't know what it is, it's—getting kind of woozy—delirious and hot, like with a bad flu—goddamn there's got to be something I can—

Come on Bo it's in the back of your mind, go ahead try praying. Go ahead!

— Yeah okay dear God please help…

Not working. Not sure what God, the one in the Duomo's Judgment Day scene I don't think so, concocted by the gentry to scare common folk into a state of ovine obedience, keep them toiling productively away, once you get them past the first level of illogic the others easier to swallow, the physical impossibilities, the miracles, the contradictions—do unto others and thou shalt not kill, set against Valverde and Pisarro's biblical slaughter, blood of a thousand Incas saturating the ground in His name at Cajamarca. And the idea that a creator would set at the apex a being hardwired to succumb to temptation and then make of his life an ongoing test of ability to resist, was it God himself who thought up this twisted practical joke, or those who wrote the book, and what of the great thinkers who refined it, were they true believers, or in on the ruse, confident they would never really be judged, free to get away with anything they could in this life...yet even the concoctors must have felt the need to revere something greater. The need a part of evolution, moving us along from lone predator to social animal, sacrificing self to greater good, maybe any God is the manifestation of that greater good, portrayed in human form, easier to grasp than some abstract concept of benevolence, we need something tangible to identify with, a king, or queen, or a movie star, or even a material dream as of how enhanced your life might be if you drive an S-class and wear a Patek Phillipe, the pervasive god of affluence worshipped even on the street with every purchase of a fake Rolex, online shoppers' hot pursuit of any name in our modern pantheon, Gucci Prado Blahnik Armani a material god for every level from Bentley to Tommy Hilfiger, is there a consumerist gene that I seem to lack, is it too part of evolution, humans randomly trying every behavior until one clicks, if so our preoccupation with self gratification would seem to be taking us backward toward the predator and maybe even farther back, the receding glacier back there evidence of a primitive inability to recognize that our compulsive burning of what's essential for life on the planet and converting to fumes is slowly but surely raising the violence of our storms and changing our soil to desert, will some future visitors to the solar system observe a few artifacts remaining in our sterile landscape and ponder that our self-inflicted demise came more recently than that of our red neighbor, are we really no more able to control our actions than the mold that encircles and consumes the orange until there is nothing left to consume, that can't be so.

That can't be so, there must be hope there must be some hope for escape from what seems inevitable both for the earth and for me, but here and now it's clear that no hope can come from chanting *nam ryoho renge kyo* for a new flatscreen tv or diving deep into Aquinas' elaborations but at times the feeling that I'm part of all that's happening on this planet is strong enough it might qualify as religious, the shared consciousness that binds us all together might if I devoted myself to it take me into a rapturous state like Bach and Vivaldi and Mozart inhabited when they were composing their most beautiful music, I might go farther into this, could start right here with these rolling waves whose rhythm has over years become part of me...other living things at hand, rockfish salmon and cod somewhere below...the occasional shearwater browsing by...Wade not far away a good and true partner, Karen, Gary, other friends in Sitka, Myra. Myra who I will never have the chance with, oh God this pursuit of prayer is only making me more and more sorrowful but God oh God please God I don't want to die.

Bo jamming bent leg against back cockpit wall

trying to take strain off. The cold sinking in further. Shivers turning to shaking, Bo unable to quell until his system protectively shuts down again.

Rocking along in the trough, the seas steady abeam. Light fading early under the thick low clouds and then disappearing altogether. The Walter a dark shape moving through the dark night.

CHAPTER 28

Weird rhythmic sound resolving into the wush-wush-wush of a big nearby screw. Growing louder. And yet louder. Hard thump as a moving wall of steel strikes the port pole. Levering the Walter's stern around to sharp contact with the ship's after end, horrendous scraping feet from Bo's head wrenching him awake the stern quarter grinding along the implacable iron face until as it curves away the Walter sucked backwards and down into a hole barely missing a huge slashing blade and shipping half a ton of propwash into her port cockpit. Bo instinctively trying to jump away. And succeeding? Huge dark shape moving away, gleam of high stern light receding into the distance.

Bo looking down at arm. Still partly stunned, standing in half full cockpit, water slowly draining through scuppers. I'm free?

Boots full, feet cold. Cold all over—move now, get into warm cabin. Can't climb up, legs not working. Lean here and wiggle feet for a few minutes. Come on blood. That's better, maybe I can haul myself up yes.

Sloshing forward to painstakingly pull boots off and enter the wheelhouse and close to stove. Oh that feels good. Let's turn it up. Jesus what happened. The wire, must have got caught between that monster whatever it was and the rail. Chafed it through. Wow.

Lay arm on table, turn overhead light on. That is ugly. Above the clamped point a vast bruise, below the fingers pale and blue. But look I can still move them a little...ow fuck that is starting to hurt *really* bad, if I elevate it helps, yeah a little but, shit shit! Almost too much—but pain's a good sign, a sign it's alive, will recover maybe? God I hope—okay, I can walk around with it in the air, get up to the autopilot, get you turned around Walter you good old boat. Attracting a savior ship, how did you do that. God I am tired. And thirsty, glug some water man that is good. Hungry too but I think I will lie down here. Get the quilt over me and....

Wakened some hours later by thirst and hunger. Swallow another pint of water, kettle's warm get a quick cup of cocoa and a pot for my best friend Dinty. I can't work the can opener. But maybe I can use my swiss army knife—yeah. Slow as hell, but, got it. Man this cocoa is good.

Stew smells exceptional. See if it's hot yet. Well no. But no sense waiting till it burns my mouth. Oh yes warm is just fine.

Could sleep more but I think we need to get on out of here. Where are we anyway, check the plotter.

Twelve miles northwest of the hambone—damn—I must've totally fucked up the calculation last night. I wouldn't have come anywhere those guys. Jesus! I must've done something good in my life to get a break like this. Okay get a course set toward Sitka. Oh, the gear's still in the water, huh. Cut the wires and take off? No, still got one good arm, I can get it in.

Back out to the scene of my recent imprisonment, get these lines on board. Take it slow, I can do it one handed. Holy shit there's a fish. With a giant munch out of its belly. Egg loving sharks know just where to bite, get the whole skein. And here's another. Walter, they think you're a damn delicatessen. Here's another—no, this one's whole, lift it aboard. Can I clean onearmed. Sure I can.

Last lead secure in holder, throttle set to half running speed, Bo pulling new sharp knife out and addressing pile of five very dead kings. Leaning on fish with right forearm, slicing more or less in the right places. And taking an occasional break to hop up and down. Simply for the joy of being able to do so.

Half an hour later Bo emerging from fish hold into the pale light of a new day. Dense cloud and drizzle. Ow this hand again throbs. Get inside speed up and refine heading. Direct course to White Sisters will take me inside the banks, can't wave to partners. But can talk at checkin time nine o'clock. Get comfy in pilot chair. Take a catnap or two as we steam along, shouldn't be any boats along here…

—Bo! Bo! You prodigal recalcitrant uncooperative excuse for a partner! Talk to me.

Startled awake. Shit I slept two hours straight.

—Wade, yeah it's me I hear you.

—You're actually out here? Not in Pelican selling a huge trip you caught in some secret spot you didn't want to share?

—No not at all. I, uh, I just kinda got wrapped up in what I was doing. Is all.

—Yeah. I hope there's more to your story than that.

—Well, actually…

The bizarre tale told, received with amazement. Request for Wade's medical advice yielding some comfort, intervention not likely needed, ibuprophen to reduce pain and swelling. Good luck and get your ass back out here soon, help us find the fish.

Bo taking this advice to heart, vitalizing with mess of fried eggs and pot of coffee. Intent to run straight through to Sitka beginning well but frustrated by rising headwinds and accompanying sharp chop.

Late evening, the Chichagof Island shore coming into dim view through rain and spray. Bo fading fast. Can't do this, I'll fall asleep and run onto some rock. Better find an anchorage, run the rest of the way tomorrow. What's nearby. Kukkan Bay. Shit it's getting dark. Won't be able to see those shoals in the entrance. But the plotter will lead us past them, radar will help. Just pay attention.

Anchor down in calm water, Bo gratefully sinking

into deep dreamless sleep. To wake early and go yawning on deck. Windless in this protected bay. No sound in misty drizzle except one occasional long sad note from thrush hidden in spruce forest. A solitary bird with apparently no friend in this gloomy world. Bo taking contemplative seat on anchor winch. Or maybe that could be the voice of God, trying to communicate his essential loneliness? Sure it would be a sad position at the top of the heap…supposing it could be true God put all this together and tried to install man in his image at the peak…if so, he blew it and produced a misfit. Or, he's just as screwed up as we are. Either way, plenty of reason for regret, which could explain him being over there in a tree sorrowfully tweeting…

Hey.

Bo.

Get real and find some other creation theory. Sure it's entertaining running all these variations, but aren't you just using them as a cover up? For the fact that, for anyone who can't make a giant illogical leap of faith, that God's not around?

There's no Dad in the sky to protect us from evil. Or to ask for a loan. Or if we can borrow the keys to the planet.

They're already ours.

Tough as it might be to admit, since it takes the responsibility off God and puts it on us. Or at least those of us who can make the easier leap of faith—that the world could be a better place, that we can affect how much evil there is, that the other things that live here merit our respect, that we're strong enough to get along without dominating or crushing them. That man is basically good. If we believe that, then there's no choice than to take on the job ourselves. And maybe that's where you find God. Inside anyone who, like Kant said, actually acts on the belief in a better world.

CHAPTER 29

Bo shifting on the galvanized steel winch housing. Occasional small riffles crossing the bay's surface. Drizzle beginning to chill. I have to take on God's responsibilities? That's intimidating. But hopeful too, in a way. Relying on someone external to do the job wasn't going all that well, seems like God lost interest and moved on quite a while ago anyhow even if he was real for some. That bird was real, but no sound from him for some time now. Not even a mournful bird for company…all alone here…okay, come on, there's good friends only a hundred miles away. But no one to love—

That dream! I forgot, damn…

Bo himself suddenly galvanized, pulling anchor and threading the protected inside passage toward Khaz through a myriad of rocky islets, turning over in mind the images of Mariella as dreamed, as remembered. Be real, isn't that how it would have played out? Why would she take to this often tedious life? Little here for anyone not appreciative of nature at its most elemental. And that wasn't her. Raised to be urbane, academics and music her preoccupations. Unimpressed even with those magnificent Mediterranean seas breaking on the rocks at Navarola, more taken with the shops, the room...the bed...her beautiful hungry body...oh Jesus why relive that. Face it—she was using me. To get over Giovanni. And when he put the moves back on, she just dropped it. Left me with sense of humor trashed, knocked off balance into a swamp of sorrow and regret I'm still trying to climb out of...the dream, focus on the dream. That's how it would have been, for sure. I am one lucky son of a bitch it was only a dream, and not my summer.

Lucky, but still alone. Except the possibility with Myra. Oh, how could I let that thing with Reilly happen. Damn I hope I didn't fuck things up permanently. It's gotta be fixable! Call her! Can't, still in middle of nowhere, no service. Damn! Come on Walter!

Vibrating with anticipation through Neva and Olga. Finally off Starrigavan Bay bars on phone. No answer on cell. Try the Watchdog. A colleague explaining, Myra gone to Juneau to cover Rick Corvis' first Board of Fish meeting, not back till late. Okay, might as well go get these fish out of the hold—Wow Rick's actually on the Board—down this rainy channel to the plant, holler up.

—Anybody up there can help me unload my fish? One of my wings doesn't work so well.

And I need to save the right one to steady my phone while fumbling keypad with the left. Still no answer.

Bo motoring back toward Thompson contemplating fish ticket. Not good but better than what I was heading for. Where would I be, two days farther, still trolling west, the Walter about to run aground on some rocky Kodiak shore, well after I'd checked out. Okay get these lines on the dock. Try the phone again, she should be home…

—Hello?

—Myra! I, I uh, I thought maybe it wasn't rainy enough here, you moved to Ketchikan—

What the hell are you saying!

—I mean, how have you been?

—Oh, Bo, what are you calling me for.

—Because, because I'm sorry we went sideways, really sorry, and I want to fix it.

—I don't think that's possible, Bo, I—

—It is! It's totally possible, if you'll give me a chance—look, I'll come over, explain in person. Just hang on five minutes, I'll be there.

—That's really not a good idea, Bo…Bo?

Bo speeding down Katlian and parking, dashing up the stairs knocking lefthanded and fidgeting expectantly. Some long moments later a voice through the door.

—You need to go away, Bo.

—Myra, come on, let me in, it's not like you thought, really.

—I'm serious Bo, I don't want to get hurt any more.

—I'm sorry you were hurt, Myra. But that thing

with Reilly, it was, like, a humanitarian thing! Not a love thing. Reilly was having this big trauma, she was really needy, I mean, almost flipping out…and, how it is, I've been kind of unhinged…I got dumped really hard last year and it's been a long slow recovery… this was a, an, an accident! With absolutely nothing to do with how I feel for you, which is—

—You're telling me, you didn't make love with her, you made 'need'? An accident? So maybe our night together was an accident. I think you'd better leave, Bo.

—No wait Myra we weren't—aren't—an accident at all. We were, totally premeditated!—and it was so, so beautiful—why don't we…we could step back a little, if you want? It feels so right with you Myra. I—we can't just give it up…what do you think?

—Myra? Hello?

—Okay, if you're still listening, please, just think it over, I'll wait while you do, just kinda…hang out here…and wait for you…

Silence. Bo moving close, leaning forehead against the door. More silence. And yet more. Forehead getting sore. Moving back to lean against rail. Silence. Shifting position. Uncomfortable standing, sink down and sit back propped against railing, arms on knees. Is she thinking about us I wonder. Doing so quietly, if she is. Going to bed, forgetting about it? I don't think so. Or hope not anyway. Jesus I'm tired. Tired enough to nod off. Maybe just curl up here in front of the door. What if a neighbor finds me. Ah well. Sitkans tolerant of odd behavior. Rug kinda thin here on this hard floor. But still. Better than sleeping outside. So, thanks for letting me use your hallway Myra. Goodnight in there.

Hours passing. Until some time after midnight. Door quietly opening. And Bo coming to consciousness as a toe softly prods his ribs. Reaching up…caressing this sweet curve of calf to ankle. Oh, Myra.

We are going to be so good together.

Afterword

West of Spencer is a work of fiction. Any resemblance of its characters to persons living or dead is entirely coincidental...save three, who are based on exceptional friends whose bright spirit enlivened my years of trolling. Two met their end way too soon while fishing, the third has started a new life an ocean away, and I miss them all. This story is dedicated to Gary, to Matt, and to Doc---you remain a huge inspiration.

Made in the USA
Charleston, SC
18 April 2013